Black Neighbor, White Wife

By J.W. McKenna

Other books by J.W. McKenna:

Out of Control 1 & 2 (anthologies)
Office Slave, Office Slave II: El Exposed
Stripped & Abused
Controlled!
Sold Into Slavery
Boarding School Slave
Tied & Branded
The Politician's Wife
My Husband's Daddy
My Wife's Master
Torn Between Two Masters
Darkest Hour
Corruption of an Innocent Girl
The Sex Slave Protocols
Secretary's Punishment
The Abduction of Isobelle
Starlet's Fall
Joanna's Surrender
Slave to the Firm
She Couldn't Say No
Lara's Submission
Remedial Sybian Training
Trailer Park Tramp
Her Personal Assistant
Kyla's Basic Training
The Cheater
Training Bra
Two Girls in Trouble
Punish the Slaves
Landlord Ladies
Trained in Two Weeks
Nude in New Zombieville
Eighteeen & Desperate
The Tutor's Dilemma
Be Careful What You Wish For: A Cuckold's Story
The Advantages of Marrying a Cuckold

Copyright, 2014, J.W. McKenna Publishing. All rights reserved. May not be reprinted without written permission from the author.

Chapter One

Barb Turner spotted the U-Haul trailer outside her apartment building when she arrived home at four-thirty.

Another sucker, she thought, recalling the lazy super who never seemed to get around to fixing anything. His attitude was: Wait long enough and the tenants will solve the problems themselves. She and her husband Dave had wanted to move out the 1930's four-story walk-up building for months but could never find another one-bedroom apartment they could afford in Brooklyn.

A hulking, bald African-American man suddenly appeared behind the glass as she walked up, giving her a start. He opened the door and stepped aside. He gave a thin smile and nodded.

"Moving in?" she asked, hoping he was just the hired help.

"Nah," he said. "My brother is, though."

Damn, Barb thought. She didn't consider herself to be racist, but it made her nervous to have scary black men moving into her building. She vowed to intensify their search for a new place. She rued the day they had left Manhattan.

"Well, welcome to the neighborhood anyway," she said, smiling through her fears. At that moment, she realized she *might* be a bit racist after all.

He nodded and headed toward the van. She went in and

picked up her mail from the box. Barb turned when she heard a footstep and nearly collided with a younger black man. He took her breath away – but not in the same way as the other man did. He was gorgeous – a young Denzel Washington-type gorgeous. Although big and muscular, he moved with a feline grace.

"Oh!"

"Sorry, ma'am," he said, smiling. "Didn't mean to scare you."

"Oh, that–that's all right." Standing this close to him had an immediate effect on her: She blushed and felt a warmth spread through her. She couldn't imagine this was the scary man's brother. "Are you moving in?"

"Yes, 3-C."

"Oh! I met your brother."

"Santana? I hope he didn't startle you too much!"

She laughed. "Oh, no… well, yeah, I guess he did, a little bit."

"Don't worry – he's actually a softie. He just looks mean. I'm Carlos." He stuck out a hand.

"It's nice to meet you," she said, taking his hand into hers. It felt warm and inviting. She guessed his age to be in his early thirties. Then the juxtaposition of the names hit her. "Uh, Carlos … and Santana?"

Carlos laughed. "Yeah, my dad was a big fan of the guy. Used to go to his concerts whenever he came to New York."

His sense of humor disarmed Barb. "I'm Barb. My husband Dave and I are right above you in 4-C." She felt it was necessary to mention she was married right away to avoid any misperceptions. Still, she couldn't deny the visceral thrill that ran through her and now seemed to center on her pussy. She was shocked at her body's response to this man.

"So if I make too much noise, you can stomp on the floor, right?"

"Yeah, right. I'd like to think I'd be more polite than

that!" She pulled her hand free and started to move away, her mind spinning. She could see him checking her out and wondered if he would be disappointed. At twenty-nine, Barb didn't consider herself to be beautiful, although she felt she had a nice body. At least, that's what Dave kept telling her. She dyed her brown hair a dark blonde, but she couldn't say she had more fun because of it.

"How is it living here?"

She paused, wondering how much to tell him. "It's okay. The super's a lazy bum and the elevator doesn't work, but otherwise, it's fine. The price is right."

He nodded. "Good to know. Well, I'd better get back to helping or my brother will get mad."

"Okay. Bye." She walked up the stairs, again cursing the landlord for not fixing the elevator. It had been broken for four months now. The super kept telling them they were waiting for parts. Yeah, if the parts had to be made in Middle Earth by gnomes and shipped by raft!

Inside her apartment, Barb dropped her purse and headed for the refrigerator. She poured herself a glass of wine and listened to the sounds of Carlos and his brother moving in below. She couldn't understand why he'd had such a powerful effect on her. She was happily married! Well, almost, anyway. Dave was a nice guy and he adored her. It wasn't his fault he wasn't a very good lover. He tended to come quickly whenever they made love, leaving her wanting. His small penis didn't help, either. She was too embarrassed to masturbate in front of him, so she would lay beside him while he dropped off to sleep, silently frustrated. She only "took care of herself" when Dave was out of the apartment.

Like now, she thought. She carried her wine into the bedroom. Dave wouldn't be home for another hour, so she had time. She put the wine glass down on the nightstand and propped the pillows against the headboard, enjoying the preparation. It was almost like a ritual. She took off her skirt and stockings and undid her garter belt. She had never liked pantyhose and refused to wear them. But her work at the art gallery required her legs to be covered, so she wore stockings. She did like the way they made her legs look.

She lay back and settled in. Barb could hear the murmur of the men's voices downstairs and the clunk of furniture being placed. She remembered the smell of Carlos and incredible *presence*. He was in good shape, from what she could tell from her brief encounter. He had been wearing a long-sleeved pullover against the March chill, but it clung in all the right places. Her hand stole down to her panties and found them to be wet.

Ohh, such a naughty girl, she thought. She wished Dave was more imaginative in bed. It might make up for his 30-second spurt if he would take more time on foreplay or offer to role-play. Barb, the younger of two daughters in their family, had a very active imagination growing up and had expected it would continue once she met Mr. Right. Dave had had all the qualities a girl looked for in a man – kind, attentive, ambitious. He was the typical "nice guy" that mothers loved. Barb's mother certainly liked him. Dave was an assistant professor at Brooklyn College, working toward tenure. She had met him when she was twenty-five and he was twenty-eight. Barb felt she had found the man with whom she wanted to raise a family. She chose to ignore the niggling little doubts she had had whenever they made love. Those things could be worked out later, she had decided. They got married one year later.

Now, four years into married life, those little problems remained – and had grown. Plus, Dave had begged off starting a family until they could be more settled. Not that they could afford a child in this economy! Neither one made much money. Maybe after Dave got tenure…

She shook those thoughts free and returned to the matter at hand. Yes, at hand, she smiled and rubbed the folds of her pussy as she recalled her encounter with the new tenant. Carlos, he had said. *Ohh, Carlos, what you do to me!* She pretended she was single and just happened to run into Carlos in the laundry room in the basement.

"Oh, I didn't see you there," she'd say.

"Well, hello," he'd respond, moving toward her, a big smile on his face.

She could imagine what he saw – a reasonably cute blonde who kept herself in good shape by regular visits to the gym. He knew he'd want her. She'd try to ease around him but he'd block her way.

"Let me take that," he'd say, plucking the basket of clothes from her grasp and placing it atop a nearby washer.

"Please," she'd protest, her pussy growing damp at his nearness to her.

He'd ignore her, of course. She wanted him to touch her, embrace her, kiss her. And he did, right on cue. It was, after all, her fantasy.

Her pussy made squishy noises as she rubbed the clit and Barb raised her knees, imagining Carlos pressing her up against the machines, using his knee to lift one of her legs. He'd reach underneath and find her to be very wet.

"Ohhh, look at you," he'd growl, "you want this."

"No," she'd say, although it wasn't true. "I should go."

"You're not going anywhere," he'd respond, ripping her panties from her body and making her gasp.

She'd struggle to no avail. He would be too strong. His fingers moved to his pants and when he unzipped himself, Barb began to rub her fingers harder against her pussy, imagining how afraid and horny she'd be, a conflicting set of emotions.

She could see him now, his hard cock thrusting up at her. There would be no where for her to go. He'd hold her in place as his penis slipped inside her.

"God, yes," Barb cried out in her bed as she pictured the

scene so clearly. His cock would be big and thick and it would reach her in places that Dave couldn't. She used her fingers as a poor substitute to maintain her fantasy. "Oh god, you're gonna make me come!"

Her knees went wider as she imagined Carlos thrusting himself deep into her again and again and she'd be helpless to stop him. Her body would be his to use and she could feel his cock swelling within her, ready to erupt at any second–

"Oh my god!" she cried and climaxed, slapping her thighs together and rolling to the side. The orgasm rocked her – she was startled by its power.

"My god," she moaned, thinking she was a bad wife for pretending she was enjoying being attacked by this new neighbor.

He's probably not like that at all, she chided herself. *He's probably just a regular nice guy!*

So why did her imagination immediately go with him being a thug and practically raping her? Was it Carlos' scary brother that brought it on? Or was it the stereotype of the black man that caused it? Either way, she'd owe Carlos a silent apology the next time she saw him.

Sorry I masturbated to you forcing yourself on me, she thought. *I know you're probably not like that at all!*

She giggled and got up and went into the bathroom to clean herself up.

Two days later, Barb ran into Carlos in the lobby and she felt her pussy grow warm and damp at the sight of him. She wondered if he could guess he had fueled an illicit fantasy. It would probably not be the last time.

"Hi," she said as he passed.

He paused. "Hi, back. Hope I'm not making too much noise for you guys."

"Oh no! Not at all. I can't hear a peep."

He smiled. "Good. Oh, and you were wrong about the

super. I had some trouble with my faucet and he came right up and fixed it."

"Really? Huh." That wasn't like Frank. "Maybe you scared him or something." The words slipped out before she thought about how it might sound. "Uh... I mean..."

He laughed. "Don't worry. Sometimes being a big black guy has its advantages."

"Yeah... I'm sorry... I didn't mean..."

"Relax, I know what you meant." He moved off down the hall and Barb let go a long, slow breath. *Great*, she thought, *now the poor guy thinks I'm some kind of racist!*

She shook her head. She probably was a racist, but in a good way. She fantasized about him fucking her and idly wondered if the rumors about black men were true. Barb suddenly felt an urge to retreat to her apartment and take care of her itch. *No, I have to get to work!*

She hurried for the door, trying to block out the images that seeped into her mind.

"Did you meet our new neighbor yet?" she asked her husband later that evening, when they were both relaxing on the couch with glasses of wine.

"The black guy? No, not yet." She had told him about Carlos, but left out any details. "What about him? Anything I should know?" Dave was a compact man who looked the part of an assistant university professor – he was short and slender, with a full head of dark hair and wire-rimmed glasses.

"No, not really. I just wondered if you'd seen him, that's all."

He shrugged. "Nope." He paused. "Is he giving you the eye or something?"

"Oh, no! He's a perfect gentleman!" She wondered if it sounded a bit forced.

"Well, that's good. Wouldn't want him stealing my wife away!"

"Oh? You think he could?" Her voice was light.

"Nah, but you know what they say…" He winked at her.

Barb played dumb. "Oh? And what do *they* say?"

He suddenly grew embarrassed. "Aww, nothin'. Forget it."

"Come on, you sound suddenly worried or something."

Dave grinned. "Well, I haven't heard too many complaints…"

She had meant to say something like, "You do just fine!" or some other reassuring line. But instead she blurted, "I'm not a complainer."

He stared at her. "Oh. That again?" Like it was *her* fault she didn't come.

"Yeah, well, you kinda brought it up."

"I know, I know! Jeez!" Now he was angry. Or maybe just embarrassed.

"Sorry. I don't want to hurt your feelings."

"So you'd rather just lay there and be frustrated?" He took a big gulp of wine.

"No! I mean… I don't do that! It's very nice!"

"You just don't come, that's all. Great."

"I enjoy our special time together, you must know that!"

"I'm not sure I do. Maybe you should try out this Carlos guy and see how a real man can make love!" Oh, he was definitely angry now, but there was embarrassment in his voice as well. Or shame.

"Stop it!" She said. "You're a great husband! It's such a small thing in the big scheme of things. Come on, honey, don't be this way!"

" 'Small thing' – ha ha. Funny. Look, it's a pretty big deal if you ask me."

"Like I said, it's a sm- I mean, it's just one aspect of who you are. I love *you*, David Turner, not just your dick!"

"Sounds like you don't love it too much! I mean, jeez!"

"This is why we don't talk about it! You always get so

defensive!" She got up and headed into the kitchen. Dave followed her at once. He grabbed her arm and spun her around.

"Wait! There were times that I remember you came!" He paused, recognition dawning on his face. "Unless you've been faking it all this time…"

She decided not to lie any more about it. "I just didn't want to hurt your feelings," she said.

"Fuck! A guy likes to know these things. I mean, fuck! We could've fixed it! We've been married four years – all this time you've been faking it?"

"I've enjoyed it! It's different for women! We like the closeness, the cuddling just as much! It's not all about coming, you know."

He shook his head. "Okay, that's it. I'm going to make it my mission to make you come, okay?"

She dimpled. "Really?"

"Of course! And I don't want to hear you pretending anymore! Okay?"

Her smile widened. "Okay."

He stuck out his hand and she shook it, an odd ritual for a married couple. Then he smiled. "Well, I think we should get started."

"Right now? We haven't even had dinner yet!"

"Fuck dinner. Come on." He grabbed her hand and dragged her down the hall.

It was nearly a disaster, Barb thought. Dave was trying too hard and could barely get an erection. When he finally did, he got so excited, he came quickly, though it was obvious he was trying to last until she came. To her credit, she didn't fake it. She just lay there while Dave groaned over her.

"Damnit!" he said. "I didn't mean to come so soon!"

"Don't worry about it," she said, scooting up against the pillows. "We can try again tomorrow." She knew he needed some time to recover.

"No, damnit! I said I'd make you come and I mean it!"

He pulled her back down on the bed and spread her legs. He dove into her pussy and began to lick her. It startled her – he hadn't given her oral sex in months.

"Hey! You don't have to do that!" Wasn't he tasting himself?

He pulled away and said, "Just tell me what feels good, okay?"

That surprised her. Was he actually going to be selfless for once? "Okay," she said, settling in. Dave began to lick her, too hard at first, but he took direction well.

"No, softer… Good. More tongue. Ahhh, that's it."

Soon he found the right rhythm and she began to feel the tendrils of an orgasm approaching.

"Oh!"

Her body language encouraged him and he kept at it. "Yes," she gasped, "Now, put a finger inside!"

He obeyed at once and Barb could feel her climax swell inside her. "Yes, yes," she cried, "Now two fingers! Yes, that's it!" In her mind, it wasn't Dave's fingers – it was Carlos's thick black cock thrusting into her. She was back in the laundry room, her hips against a machine, Carlos pressed tightly against her. Oh yes! The image accelerated her climax. "Oh god! I'm gonna come! Oh!"

Suddenly, her legs jerked and she crested into her orgasm. Her thighs slapped together around Dave's head and she cried out and pushed him away, her pussy suddenly too sensitive for his rough tongue.

"Oh my god! Oh fuck!"

When she calmed down, she looked up to see Dave grinning at her. "See, I told you!" He seemed quite pleased with himself.

"Wow! That was… that was great!"

"Happy to help. So I trust you won't be faking it any more?"

"Hell no! I mean, that was … very nice!"

"Good." He rolled off the bed and got up. She noticed his cock was quite limp. "Let's eat."

She could hardly move. "Uhh, you go ahead. I need to rest."

"That's okay. I'll whip up something. I'll let you know when it's ready." He left, a jaunty lilt to his step.

Barb just lay there for several minutes, marveling at her husband's new attitude. If it would only last, she mused. She could remember, back when they had first started dating, Dave would give her oral sex on a regular basis. All that had faded once they had gotten married. Was he turning over a new leaf?

Chapter Two

Barb had hoped Dave's new-found desire to give her the climaxes she needed would continue, but he soon lost interest. He was "too tired" after he came himself and would drop off to sleep, leaving her frustrated. Rather than let it go, she confronted him about it.

"Hey!" She said when he rolled off of her after a recent attempt at love-making. "What about all your promises?"

"Oh... I'm sorry, honey. I'll do better next time – I promise." He gave her a small smile and rolled over, his back to her.

"Okay, that's it!" she said.

He turned his head and looked a bit worried. "What's it?"

"You don't get to come first any more!"

"Well, that might be hard to arrange. I mean, it just happens, you know?" He tried to get back to the business of sleeping, but she wouldn't have it.

"It won't happen if you don't get to put your penis in my body!"

"Wait – what?"

"You heard me! From now on, when we make love, I get to come first or we don't fuck!"

He was taken aback by her forcefulness. "Jeez, okay! Now let me sleep, please."

"Enjoy it while you can," she told him.

She was true to her word. A week later, when Dave cuddled up to her in bed, she encouraged him. But when he rolled her over on her back and tried to climb on, she raised a knee into his stomach.

"Omph! Ow! Hey!"

"You don't get to come first, remember?"

"Ohh. Rrrright." He seemed to be thinking about whether he wanted to continue.

"Hey, it's okay with me if you don't ever want to make love again. But this is the way it's going to be. Remember all your promises about doing better?"

"Yeah, yeah. I'm sorry. Okay." He bent down and began to lick her moist cleft. She settled in and waited, but she could tell his heart wasn't in it. He was just doing the minimum job necessary to get her off. It wasn't working.

"Hey!" she said. "You're not trying very hard."

"Sorry. Look, maybe if I could just…" He rubbed his hard cock against her thigh.

"No! If you keep this up, maybe I'll have to find another man to fuck me!"

He paused at looked up at her. "Really?"

"Yeah – Carlos is starting to look pretty good right about now!"

He laughed. It surprised her that he didn't get angry. He seemed almost titillated by the idea.

"Okay, okay!" He returned to his task and soon had her rising toward an orgasm.

"That's better," she murmured. "Oh yes."

Once again, she imagined it was Carlos going down on her – and now he was going to fuck her. "Use your finger," she told Dave and he obeyed. No, too thin, she decided. She was sure Carlos's cock was much bigger. "Use two." Oh, yes, that was better. "Oh god…"

She could picture Carlos above her, his thick cock reaching inside her. "Yes!," she gasped and Dave slipped another finger inside her. "Faster! Yes! Oh my god!" She crested into her orgasm and squeezed her thighs around Dave's head. She collapsed onto the bed and Dave immediately moved up over her. She smiled and let him have his way. She could barely feel him as he slipped inside her. After a few pumps, he groaned and stopped moving, resting his weight on her. She hugged him and said, "Now, that was sooo much better!"

He grunted his acquiescence.

* * *

The elevator had been fixed! Barb stood staring at it, not sure she believed it. All the signs were down and it opened invitingly at the touch of the button. Did she dare get on? Would she wind up as some sort of terrible experiment, trapped for days? She took a deep breath and stepped on. She pushed one. The doors closed and the elevator began to move. Suddenly, it stopped and she felt her worst fears were about to be realized. Then the doors opened and Barb was felt a wave of relief and heat wash over her when she spotted Carlos standing there, dressed in a suit and tie. "Oh, hi," she said, feeling her pussy grow damp as soon as he stepped inside.

"Hi. I thought you said the elevator was broken."

"It was! They must've fixed it." She smiled, thinking about how he had helped her climax when her husband had made love to her last night.

"You look like the cat that swallowed the canary," he remarked.

"Oh, sorry. I'm just in a good mood, that's all."

"That's a good way to be. You going to work?"

"Yeah. I work at the Corridor Gallery on Grand," she said. "How about you?"

"Yeah, I'm heading to my job at Charles Schwab."

"Oh! You're a stock broker!" She was pleased. Not only handsome, but rich too!

"Yeah, but I'm just one of the lowly grunts. I'm still in

training."

"Still, I imagine that takes quite a bit of smarts to do that job."

He shrugged. "Maybe. We'll see."

This close, she could smell his manly odor and it made her grow wetter. She worried he could smell the scent of her arousal. Thankfully, they reached the bottom floor and the doors opened.

He turned toward her. "Well, have a nice day." He walked ahead.

It took Barb a few seconds to compose herself before she could leave the lobby. It amazed her that Carlos could have such a powerful effect on her. If he only knew about his secret role in improving her sex life!

It's about fucking time, she thought.

Dave made overtures to her after dinner on Saturday. Barb wasn't really in the mood because she had taken care of herself Friday afternoon, before he arrived home from work, once again using Carlos as her imaginary lover. Still, she felt it was her "wifely duty" so she allowed herself to be talked into bed early. This time, he didn't object when she asked that he take care of her needs first.

He's learning.

She thought she should feel guilty about using Carlos as a crutch to reach her orgasm, but in the moment, anything was fair game. Dave was a good man and all, but he didn't light the fire under her like Carlos did. That was probably because Carlos was off limits and it made it all the more illicit. As he licked her warm cleft, she again pretended it was Carlos between her legs, prepping her before shoving his thick cock into her. She could picture it, even though she had never seen it. She just knew it would be a hefty specimen. Black men were like that, weren't they?

"God, use your fingers!" she gasped at Dave and he

obliged. She quickly rose toward her climax. "Oh god! Yes! Fuck!"

She sank back into the bed, legs akimbo, satisfied once again. Dave moved up over her. She lay basking in the glow while Dave rutted on top of her. It was over in two minutes. He rolled to the side and promptly went to sleep. Barb used a tissue to clean herself up and wondered what it might be like to make love to a man like Carlos for real. It made for some satisfying dreams.

Sunday morning, after breakfast, Barb decided to pop down to the laundry room to see if the machines were free. There were only three washers and two dryers to service the entire apartment building of sixteen units, so finding a machine free was a hit and miss affair. Fortunately, many of the tenants had given up and started taking their clothes down the street to the laundrymat. Maybe she would get lucky.

She pulled on some shorts and a T-shirt and took just one basket down, thinking if she could find another machine free, she'd run upstairs and grab the other one. She was pleasantly surprised to find no one there and all the machines empty.

"Cool!" she said aloud and quickly filled one washer and started the load. Barb was about to head up to get the other basket when the door opened and Carlos entered, wearing sweat pants and a Giants jersey and carrying a laundry basket. She froze, remembering her daydream and felt herself suddenly grow hot.

He caught her stare and her rigid demeanor.

"Hope I'm not bothering you," he said, moving toward a machine.

"Uh… no! I mean… Sorry, you just startled me, that's all."

"Well, I'll be out of your hair in just a minute." He filled the machine.

Barb shook herself out of her reverie. "Uh… Do you

need both machines?"

"No, this should be good." He paused. "Are these machines kept pretty busy?"

"Uh…" *Why couldn't she stop saying that!* "Sometimes. Some people just take their laundry down to that place on 14th Avenue," she said. "I mean, it's not like they could fit any more equipment in this tiny room!" She laughed, a forced sound that made her feel like an idiot. He gave her a strange look. He started the machine and added soap and flashed her a quick smile.

"Well, I'll check back later on this." He started to leave.

Barb worried that he thought her to be afraid of him or worse, racist. She spoke up before he could reach the door.

"Wait."

He turned. "Yes?"

"I, uh, think I owe you an apology."

He tipped his head. "Why?"

"Well, when you and your brother were moving in, I was… um… afraid and I think that was just a reaction to not being around too many black guys or something," she said lamely, thinking she was just making it worse.

"Really? You were afraid of me?"

"Well, not you so much, but your brother, yeah."

He nodded and smiled. "He can have that effect on people. I think it's the shaved head."

"Yeah. Anyway, I just wanted to say sorry if I seemed to have had a deer-in-the-headlights look that first day."

"No problem. You seem to have recovered well." He turned toward the door.

Barb felt a sudden urge not to let this moment pass. "There's more."

He turned back, one eyebrow raised and waited.

She realized she had put herself in a corner and wasn't sure why she had done it. Did she really want to tell him the truth? "I was, um, nervous, just now, when you showed up, but not for the same reason."

"Really? Then why?"

"I … uh… had this… uh… fantasy – or maybe dream… about you and me in this laundry room and when you came in, I … uh… froze up, I guess." Her face was hot and she wondered why in hell she had tried to explain herself.

Suddenly he smiled and nodded. He put the laundry basket down and moved toward her. Barb shrank back, her butt hitting a washing machine. He came close and filled her vision. If she wasn't afraid of him before, she was now. And her pussy was suddenly very wet.

"Let me guess," he said softly. "You imagined how it might happen, you and me alone in this room. A white woman and a black man – and all the stereotypes that go with that." He grinned. "Maybe sex with your husband doesn't do it for you, hmm?"

Barb's mouth opened and closed but no sound came out.

"If you're wondering about me, I can tell you that in my case, the rumors about black men are true. And I personally believe that every white woman should experience the sensation of … let's say 'fullness' … at least once in their lives, don't you?"

"Uh…" was all she could manage.

He smiled and moved closer. She pressed herself back against the machine and worried that maybe he really meant to have sex with her. That wasn't part of her fantasy. Well, it was, but not like this!

"Please," she squeaked.

"Don't worry, I'm not a thug. I mean, unless you like that sort of thing. Some girls do. No, I just want to give you some ammunition for your next fantasy session," he said, pressing his body up against hers. She could feel his semi-hard cock against her stomach and she gasped.

"Please," she said again.

"Now imagine that you, the innocent wife, have come

down here to the laundry room and the big bad black man is here," he said, easing his body down until the shaft of his cock rubbed against her pussy. He grew harder and she couldn't believe how thick it felt. Her mouth came open. "And he's strong and powerful and you can't do anything to stop him from taking advantage of you. Your little fists beat against his chest to no avail."

She put her hands against his chest, trying to push him away, but he was a solid mass of muscle and could not be budged. She tried to ignore the warmth spreading from her loins and the thick smell of her arousal.

"I'll ... I'll call for help," she said.

He gave her a slow smile. "Hey now, this is just for the fantasy, right? None of this is really happenin'. Anyway, as I was sayin', the big bad black man pins you down and forces you to have an orgasm against your will." His cock was fully erect now and she could feel it rubbing against her clit. She felt she might actually come and worried it would only inflame him.

The sensations rose up from her stomach to her chest to her face and she could feel the heat. She began to make tiny panting noises in her throat. She wanted him to stop but she wanted him to continue as well.

What was wrong with her?

Barb couldn't seem to delay the orgasm that was building inside her against her will. It was wrong, it was dangerous, but she couldn't help it. She wanted it. She needed him to keep rubbing up against her, driving her crazy with lust…

Suddenly, Carlos pulled back and grinned. "There. How's that?" She gasped, not believing that he would stop now.

"Huh, uh…" she stammered. In her head, she was screaming, *Don't stop now!*

He picked up his laundry basket and headed for the door. "If you'd like some more material for your fantasy, just let me know." He checked his watch. "I'll be back in about forty minutes to put the clothes in the dryer." He left.

She clutched her chest, furious and relieved. If he had made her come, she doubted she could've stopped him if he had wanted to fuck her. It would not have been an assault, she realized. She would've wanted to feel his cock inside her. Her first real black cock, thick and powerful. The thought made her shiver and immediately felt guilty and she shook he head.

"Damnit."

She hurried upstairs to get the other load of laundry. His last words echoed in her head, *I'll be back in about forty minutes to put the clothes in the dryer.* He had said it on purpose, giving her an opportunity to be there when he returned. She knew what would happen if she did, so as soon as she put the load in the remaining washer, she returned upstairs and didn't go back down until an hour later.

She breathed a sigh of relief when she found she was alone in the laundry room. She quickly put her clothes in the dryer and returned upstairs, looking over her shoulder as she left, fearful and yet strangely excited.

Chapter Three

Barb didn't get a chance to apply her laundry room experience to her fantasy until Monday, when she returned from work to their empty apartment. She was pleased to have some alone time before her husband arrived home. She poured herself a glass of wine and took it into the bedroom, her mind already working.

Carlos had been right – the events in the laundry room gave her a whole new perspective on their imagined tryst. He was still strong and he still overpowered her, but it couldn't be called an assault. No, this time she was complicit in the fantasy. In her imagination, she would encourage him by wearing a short skirt and a thin blouse down to the laundry room, using the excuse that she had no clean clothes. Carlos would come in and see her. He'd be wearing the same outfit he had on Sunday, sweats and a football jersey. There would be no conversation, he would simply put down his basket and approach her.

Mirroring real life, she'd shrink back against the machine, protesting and threatening to call the cops. He'd ignore her and press himself against her body, making her gasp when she felt his hard cock. He was too tall, so he'd grab her around the waist and pull her up to sit on the washer before pulling her toward him until her butt was at the very edge. She could feel the vibration of the machine on her bottom and his big cock rubbing her clit and it would be heaven.

Barb's hand was busy between her legs, the wine forgotten on the bedside table. Her panties were already soaked.

Carlos wouldn't be satisfied with the clothes in the way. He'd roughly pull her skirt up and press his cock against her panties. One layer less material made a lot of difference and she imagined she could feel the veins on his cock.

"Please," she'd say, trying to hold onto her dignity. "I'm married."

"To a little-dicked white boy who can't give you what you need," he'd say. "You need this, I know you do."

In her fantasy, she'd nod, even though she knew it was wrong. "It's not right," she'd say anyway, giving away her conflicting emotions.

"Feels right to me." He'd pull the front of his sweatpants down and now his hard cock was naked against her panties. She imagined she could feel every bump and guessed he'd be uncut, unlike most of the men she had dated in her life. He began to rub and she felt her body shaking.

Barb gasped, her fingers squelching against her clit, her eyes shut tight.

Carlos kept rubbing his shaft against her, driving her mad. His other hand came around and pulled her tighter against him. She was going to come, she knew it and she didn't care how wrong it was.

Then, just like in real life, Carlos pulled away, leaving her gasping. Her own fingers betrayed her by lifting off of her clit to torment herself. Her body shook.

"What?" she'd say, practically pleading with her eyes for him to continue.

"You have to take your panties off yourself," he'd tell her. "That way I know you want it."

She'd be torn, wanting to come and wanting to remain faithful to her husband. Of course, in her fantasy, it was a non-issue. She wiggled out of them and let them drop to the dirty floor of the laundry room.

On the bed, Barb's hands went to her panties and slipped them off and tossed them on the rug. Her fingers returned to her clit and her mind returned to her fantasy.

Carlos would grin at her acquiescence and his hand would force hers to feel his cock. It would be just as she remembered it from their brief encounter: long, thick – and very warm. She'd stroke it and want it inside her. He'd tease her for a few more minutes, rubbing it against her pussy until it was wet with her juices.

"Looks like someone's horny," he'd say and she'd nod.

"My husband can't make me come," she'd confess. "I need a big cock like yours."

"Of course," he'd say and slip the tip inside her.

Her mouth came open as she imagined how it might feel. She used two fingers, then three to give her the sensation and found the angle was all wrong. She put her fantasy on hold for a moment and grabbed her favorite dildo from her nightstand.

Now, where was I?

Barb jacked the toy back and forth as her imagination returned to the scene in the laundry room. She wouldn't be satisfied with the tip – and neither would Carlos. She'd scoot forward to take it all in just as he would thrust himself deep inside her. The thought of it, combined with the stroking of the dildo, made spots appear behind her eyelids. Her body shook, her mind reeled, her mouth came open.

"Ohhhhh, fuck! Oh my god!" she cried out, her legs shaking as the climax hit her. It was like a thunderclap, rocking her body with sudden power. "Oh my fucking god!" she gasped.

When she calmed down, she knew she wasn't finished. Her mind returned to the laundry room and Carlos's cock and she did it all over again until she crested into a second orgasm. She didn't feel guilty, either. It had been too long since she had come like that. Now she realized just how much she had missed it.

Tuesday night, Barb took the initiative, something she rarely did. She knew where it came from – her pussy was still purring from Monday's fantasy. She was ready for more. She gave him all the non-verbal clues: Touching his shoulder when she brought him a drink, hugging him for no reason and kissing him as they got ready for bed. He seemed oblivious.

"Honey?" she finally said when they were getting ready for bed. "I'm… uh, feeling kinda in the mood for some closeness…"

"Oh," he said, his face twitching. "I'm kinda tired."

"That's okay," she told him. "Just give me one quick orgasm and then you can go to sleep."

"Aw, dear, jeez, I'd love to, but I was hoping just to crash, you know?"

She narrowed her eyes. "Guess I'll have to get it somewhere else, then."

He was instantly alert. "What?"

"If you won't help me when I need it, I guess I'll ask someone else. That Carlos guy looks pretty buff – I'll bet he'd give me a good orgasm! And he probably wouldn't have to use his tongue, either."

"Hey, now, you wouldn't really do that, would you?"

"Maybe. Maybe not. But think about it, Dave – just about every time you've wanted some nookey, I've gone along, whether I was in the mood or not, just to keep you happy. Now I want some attention and you're too tired."

"You've been tired before! I don't always get my way!"

"Fine. Be that way." She rolled over and tried to get to sleep.

"Wait, wait!" he said. He pulled one of her legs toward him and bent toward her pussy.

She smiled and decided to make him work for it. "I dunno," she told him, "I'm kinda out of the mood now."

"No, don't be that way!" He began to lick her and she acquiesced, spreading her legs for him. He had been taught well over the last few weeks and soon she felt the stirrings of an orgasm rising. She returned to her favorite fantasy, Carlos. Only this time, he was licking her before he'd stick his hard cock into her. She shivered with delight as her climax neared.

"Oh yes, honey, that's good. You're such a good pussy licker," she cooed. "Use your fingers too."

Dave obliged and Barb could imagine it was Carlos' cock inside her. Dave licked harder, driving her wild. Her body began to shake and she rode that feeling until the last minute. When her orgasm exploded within her, she felt a new-found sense of power over her husband. It made it all the more delicious.

When he pulled up, he climbed over her, his little cock twitching. She put a hand on his chest. "Sorry, honey, but I'm too tired." She knew she sounded bitchy, but in the moment, she didn't care.

"Hey! I did what you asked, come on!"

"But you were too tired, remember? So let's go to sleep." She rolled away from him and ignored him as he sat on the bed, stewing.

"But I'm not tired now!" he pouted.

She sighed and turned over onto her back. "Okay, but hurry up. I'm fading fast."

Dave climbed on her and rutted for a few minutes until he groaned his release. She hardly felt him. He climbed off and gave her a peck on the cheek and moved to his side of the bed. She didn't like the sticky feeling afterward and wiped up the mess up with tissues.

It was fun, toying with her husband, but ultimately unsatisfying. Her dreams – and her daydreams – were consumed with Carlos and how his cock had felt as it had rubbed up against her. She wondered if she might accidentally run into him again. And yes, in the laundry room, which was no longer a dingy place of toil. Now it was a place for a tryst. The thought sent shivers down her back.

Barb started making extra trips to the laundry room in the basement, hoping to catch Carlos down there. But weeks went by and she never saw him. Was she just missing him or had he started taking his dirty clothes to the laundrymat two blocks away? Would he really do that? Tease her and then drop her?

At the same time she hoped to run into him, her guilt told her what she was doing was terrible and she should be glad she never saw him. *That will lead to nothing but trouble!* she told herself, sounding not unlike her mother.

A month later, in late April, she couldn't stand it. It was a Saturday morning and Dave had already left to go play softball with some friends. Without conscious thought, she found herself putting on a skirt and old blouse, instead of her usual jeans and T-shirt. She grabbed a basket of clothes and went down in the elevator one floor. She got out and rang the bell to Carlos' apartment.

He answered at once, dressed in his familiar sweatpants but no shirt. His muscles made her stomach do flip-flops. He raised his eyebrows when he saw her.

"I'm going to go do laundry," she said and started to turn away. It was all the hint she was going to give him. Even as she spoke the words, her body tingled with a mixture of arousal and guilt.

"Wait!" he called and she turned back.

"Do you have to do it right now? I was just sitting down to a cup of coffee and some eggs. You hungry?"

Everything in her mind told her not to go into his apartment. But her body moved toward the door anyway. He stepped aside and she slipped past. His apartment was a mirror of hers, but he had decorated it like a frat boy-cum-stockbroker. Posters of black basketball players and framed jerseys hung on the walls, mixed with modern furniture and lamps. An old pizza box sat on the coffee table and she could see some video game controllers out.

At the small kitchen table, he had a plate of scrambled eggs and a cup of coffee sitting out.

"I should let you eat," she said.

"No! Please, stay. Would you like some eggs?"

"No, I ate."

"How about some coffee then?"

She nodded and he poured her a cup. She put down her laundry basket, her mind screaming at her that there was a big difference between her fantasies and this reality, but she couldn't seem to help herself. Barb distracted herself by taking a sip of the coffee. It was strong and it calmed her.

"Please," she told him. "Eat before your food gets cold."

He sat down and took a bite. "Tell me how your fantasies are going."

That was a bit presumptuous, she thought. "I don't think that's any of your business."

"Oh, I think it is – otherwise, you wouldn't have rung my door, right?"

She shrugged with one shoulder. "I'm not sure why I did that." Oh, she was sure all right!

"I know why. I'll bet you've been going down to the laundry room hoping to catch me down here."

"Why haven't you been?" The words came out before she realized it just confirmed his premise.

He grinned. "I have been – but I guess I don't wash my clothes as often as you do."

She nodded, feeling foolish. This was a bad idea. "I should go." She put down her cup.

"No, please. I'm almost finished." He quickly finished his eggs. Barb wasn't sure why she stayed. Nothing but trouble could come of this.

"Tell me about your husband. What's his name again?"

"Dave. What do you want to know?"

"Well, I already know he doesn't satisfy you. Tell me how you're getting along without what you need and what you want to do about it."

"I'm not sure that's any of your business," she repeated.

He put down his fork and leveled his gaze at her. "Look, lady, you came to me." His voice hardened and it sent shivers down her spine. There was a delicious *masculine* quality to it that Dave's voice lacked. "You have some unresolved issues. I'm trying to help. But don't play coy with me. I think we're beyond that, don't you?"

She tipped her head. "Maybe. I don't know."

"So tell me. Think of me as your shrink. What's going on?"

Barb bit her lip. "Uhhhh…" Could she really tell this man about her fantasies? Wouldn't that expose her most intimate self? "I'll admit I've had some fantasies that have been, um, helpful in some ways and not in others."

He nodded. "I thought so. They've stirred up emotions. You think of yourself as a good wife, but you hate the idea of going through the rest of your life without ever experiencing a real cock, right?"

He was right but she couldn't admit it. His words were so direct, so crude. She just stared at him. "I…" She could say no more.

He rose and picked up his plate and put it in the sink. When he turned back around, her eyes went to the front of his pants and she saw the bulge there. Her heart beat faster.

"Um… could you put on a shirt?" She was trying to hang on to her marriage and his muscled chest didn't help.

He smiled. "Hey, I'm just relaxin' in my own apartment here."

"I should go." She rose.

"Wait."

She stopped, her body trembling.

"Wouldn't you at least want to see it before you go?"

Her mouth came open. She could barely breathe. She shook her head and hoped he'd ignore her.

Carlos leaned casually against the sink, a sly grin on his face. With one hand, he reached down and tugged the waistband of his sweatpants down slowly. Barb began to back away, afraid to see it. But as more of his thick cock came into view, her feet stopped and she felt frozen. Not in fear – it was more curiosity and lust. She knew she could make it to the door before Carlos reached her, if he was of a mind to act. Then she thought: Did part of her *want* him to? Did she want him to force her, just like in her fantasy?

God, she realized, *I do.*

It would take the sin out of the decision. She could claim to be the helpless victim. But she knew Carlos would never do that. Fantasies like hers didn't involve the police. Reality did. She was on a razor blade of good versus bad. Leave and I'm the good wife, sentenced to a life of dull sex. Stay and I'm the bad wife who would experience orgasms like she'd never had before.

Can't I have it both ways?, she wondered.

His cock was suddenly freed from his pants and it bounced into view, thick and long and *gorgeous*. She had been wrong about one thing – he was circumcised and it made it more attractive to her, if that was possible. It wasn't scary huge and for that she was grateful. It just seemed... the right size to her. Barb felt her mouth open as if she wanted to taste it, feel it on her tongue, against her lips. It would fit in her mouth and she would welcome it. She remembered the last time she had given Dave a blowjob. His small cock slipped easily in her mouth and he had come quickly. She had spit out his seed, as if it had tasted foul, but she couldn't recall it tasting of anything at all. Carlos's cock, on the other hand, would be *memorable*.

"Come here," he said and his voice had a commanding tone that made her want to obey him.

She stayed where she was for a moment, still torn.

"Come here," he said again, adding: "I won't bite."

She began to move toward him. She stopped five feet away, her eyes locked on his cock. It twitched and stiffened, rising up to point at her. It excited her to know that she was turning him on. "Go ahead, touch it. Just so you can say you did."

She took another step forward and reached out as if her hand was no longer obeying her mind. Or maybe it was. But she couldn't help herself – she had to touch it.

Just touch it and see what all the excitement is about, she told herself. *Then I can go home and take care of myself.*

Her fingers grasped the thick tool and she had to withhold a gasp. It felt just as good as it looked, warm and inviting. She hefted it.

"It's big," she whispered.

"It's about average," he said, "for a black man."

"But why…" She wasn't sure if she should ask.

"Why what?"

"Why are you circumcised?" Maybe he was Jewish?

He grinned. "My mom was a nurse and she felt the foreskin allowed, uh, problems to occur later, so she had it done. I'm glad. It's cleaner this way, don't you think?"

She nodded. "It's so … *thick.*"

"You've only been with white guys, so it's not surprising. Now you know why so many white girls have black boyfriends."

She nodded, willing herself to let it go and get out, but her hand refused. It hefted it and gently squeezed it and it suddenly occurred to her she might be hurting him.

"Sorry," she said, dropping it. "I don't mean to be so rough." Her hand tingled.

"You're not rough, not at all." His hand took hers and returned it to his cock. "Squeeze it, feel it grow."

She did and gasped aloud – it grew harder in her hand.

"My god, it's getting bigger!"

He laughed, a throaty sound that sent shivers through her

body. "A pretty girl does have that effect on it."

She was flattered by the compliment. Her hand squeezed it again and she marveled at how masculine it seemed. Not at all like Dave's....

The thought of her husband made the guilt return. She dropped it and stepped back. "I should go..."

"Sure," he said, "it's up to you. But I think you should at least kiss it first, just so you can say you tasted a black cock once in your life."

Barb nodded as if it made perfect sense. Her husband seemed to fade away into the background, like an annoying noise that one gets used to. She felt her knees grow weak and she sank down until she was eye level with this magnificent appendage.

"How... how big is it?"

"Only about seven-and-a-half inches. But it's pretty thick around."

"My god! I don't think I could handle anything ... like that!"

He chuckled. "You'd be surprised. The pussy is an amazin' organ."

She smiled at the thought. His cock had started to soften and she didn't want it to do that – she liked it better when it responded to her. She grasped it again and felt it stir in her hand.

"Just kiss the tip," he said and she nodded.

She opened her mouth and let her tongue touch the mushroom-shaped head. He had just showered, she could tell, and was grateful. Barb pulled back.

Okay, you've tasted it, now get up and go home!

"You can do better than that," he said in that deep, commanding tone of his and she immediately found herself agreeing with him. Her mouth returned and this time, she took more of the head inside, running her tongue around the edge. It was an amazing sensation and it caused her pussy to leak into her panties.

Once again her mind cleared and she was shocked at what she was doing. She pulled back and stood up, dizzy with conflicting emotions.

"I ... I can't do this – I have to go."

She fled and didn't look back. But she heard Carlos' dry chuckle before the door closed behind her. She made it back to her apartment before she realized she had left her basket of clothes there.

Oh fuck! Now what?

Should she go back and get them immediately? She feared what might happen if she did. Her fantasy might come true, right there in his kitchen. Should she leave them there until later, when she was more composed? She feared Carlos might go through her dirty clothes, smelling the panties and jerking off.

Fuck!

She took the stairs in order to compose herself. When she rounded the corner, she was shocked – and rather disappointed – to find her laundry basket sitting outside his door.

Huh.

Carlos was being a gentleman, she realized. If she was going to cheat on her husband, it would have to be her decision. He wouldn't force it – unless she wanted him to. And a big part of her wanted to be forced. She wanted the decision to be taken out of her hands. Looking at it from Carlos' point of view, she knew he had to protect himself. She could feel his bridled power, waiting to be unleashed. But she would have to give the word.

Barb grabbed her clothes and hurried down into the basement. It was deserted, thank god. She didn't think she could face anyone right now. She put the load into a machine, her mind spinning with what had just happened.

My god, I just put another man's cock into my mouth! What a slut!

She shivered at her close call. What had she been thinking? It had been so dangerous to knock on his door so brazenly! Like she had no control over her libido or something.

"Sometimes I just get in a mood," she said aloud.

She heard a noise and whirled around, shocked to see Carlos coming in, carrying a basket of clothes. Her mouth came open. He had at least put on a shirt, but all she could think about was his big black cock that she had just seen – and tasted.

He shrugged. "Don't mind me. I decided it was time for me to do some laundry." He grinned at her.

Barb didn't know what to say. So soon after her close call, she wasn't sure she could handle it.

"Uh… I'll be done soon."

He put his basket down on the table and approached her. She shrank back against the machine.

"Now, no need for drama, cutie," he cooed. "We both know what's goin' on here."

"I don't… I can't…"

"You can't tease a black man and not expect him to follow up," he said, pressing himself against her body. His cock was hard against her stomach and it clouded her mind. She could taste him again and she licked her lips.

He reached behind her to close the lid of the washer. Effortlessly, he picked her up and she gasped when he set her down on top. It was just like in her fantasy!

"Please! I can't!"

"Don't worry, I'm not a thug, although I am tempted," he said and she immediately felt a rush of relief. "But I am going to make you come." Her brief relief vanished, replaced by fear and excitement.

"I can't… I'm married!"

"I won't violate your marriage vows," he promised.

How could he pull that off? she wondered. It disarmed her, so she didn't object when his hands pulled her ass closer and his cock began to rub against her pussy. She groaned and put a hand against his chest. "Please..."

"Shhh," he said and kept rubbing – even, slow movements that made her quiver.

Barb was nearly lost now to her lust and she fought to maintain control. "You... said you wouldn't..." She couldn't finish.

"I won't," he said and she gave in to the sensations. After all, her skirt was in the way, plus her panties. She was safe, she told herself.

At that moment, one of his hands stole down and pulled her skirt up. Now his hard cock was rubbing against her clit, separated only by his sweatpants and her panties. She knew what would happen next. He reached down and tugged his pants out of the way, leaving his bare cock against the thin material. Barb closed her eyes. She was stunned that events could so closely follow her fantasy. It was hard to convince herself that this was really happening, that she wasn't home in her own bed, using her fingers. When she opened her eyes, she knew it was all too real.

"We can't..." she said again.

"Shhhh," he repeated. "You need this, even if it's just once. Don't you agree?"

She did, although she hated to admit it. If her husband was a better lover, she wouldn't be in this position, she told herself. Somehow that justified her decision to stay a little longer. Then again, it wasn't as if she had any choice. She liked being helpless – or maybe impossible to resist. Barb pressed her hands against his chest, as if signaling her objection, but he ignored it as she had hoped he would.

"Oh god," she gasped, feeling an orgasm stir deep within her. She couldn't do this – could she? Her mind was torn.

"Let it go," he said and it was just the right thing to say at the right moment.

Barb found herself giving up her scolding conscience and

opened herself to the sensations rolling up from her pussy. "God..." she breathed. She was close now and instead of pushing on his chest, her hands slipped around his upper arms to pull him closer to him. Carlos tightened his grip on her bottom, pulling her off the machine and hard up against him. She was rubbing directly against his shaft now and suddenly, she wished her panties weren't in the way.

She knew, if they weren't, his cock would instantly plunge into her. Is that what she wanted?

"Ah, ah, ah," she gasped, and her mind faded away. She was all pussy and it felt wonderful! She became a beast, rubbing back against him and throwing her head back. She heard noises and realized they were hers, a guttural song of sex. Her body trembled – her orgasm was coming now and she couldn't stop it, she didn't want to stop it. Suddenly, her climax erupted within her and she cried out and held Carlos tight to her. They clung together for a few seconds, her world spinning around her.

She felt him put her down on the edge of the machine and he reached around with one hand to tug the gusset of her panties aside and her conscience returned, full-force.

"I can't!" she said.

"You can't tease a black man," he responded. So much for not violating her marriage vows! A second later, she felt the bulbous head of his cock against her unprotected opening.

She tried to wriggle free, but it only caused the tip to slide into her wetness and she gasped from the thickness of it.

"We can't," she tried one last time and then his cock was inside her, spreading her apart like nothing she'd ever felt before. She threw her head back and groaned and tipped her hips up to welcome him. He responded by thrusting more of himself into her, going impossibly deep.

"Fuck! Oh my god! You're so big!"

Carlos grunted in response and began to stroke his thick cock within her. She could feel every inch of it, the veins rubbing against the walls, sending new waves of pleasure rolling up through her body until they reached her brain. She was lost and she didn't care.

As he stroked, her pussy seemed to purr and Barb understood what women saw in their black lovers. Sex would never be the same after this.

She heard a noise and looked over his shoulder to see a middle-aged woman enter the laundry room, carrying a basket of clothes. Barb gasped in shock and tried to pull back, but Carlos only pulled her tighter against him. The woman's eyes widened and she quickly stepped back and shut the door.

"Stop! Someone saw us!" she cried, but he ignored her. He kept stroking himself deeper and deeper inside her and Barb pushed aside her fears and hoped her husband wouldn't find out.

The sensations rolling up from her pussy wouldn't allow her to dwell on her guilt. She loved this man's cock! She felt her first orgasm swell and burst inside her, causing a near swoon, but he didn't stop. His cock forced another climax and she found herself biting his shoulder like some kind of wild animal. Her orgasms seemed to roll over her, one after another. She wanted to feel him erupt inside her, to accept his powerful seed like a woman should.

But he kept thrusting, his cock going even deeper. Her orgasms made her lose her mind and her body became a ragdoll in his arms. She abandoned herself to him and it freed her from guilt, at least for the moment. She didn't care if the neighbor returned to watch, bringing her friends with her.

"Fuck! Fuck! Fuck!" she gasped, her hands rising to grasp him around the neck, her legs wrapping around his narrow waist.

Her actions seemed to spur Carlos on and he was like a bull, rutting into her, his fingers like talons on her ass, driving himself into her again and again. Barb didn't think she could come any more, her entire body seemed electrified.

Suddenly, he stiffened and thrust himself hard inside her. She felt his cock give long, slow jerks and she knew he was coming. It triggered a final, deep and satisfying climax and she clung to him as he spewed his seed into her womb. They held each other tightly while his cock spurted once more.

At last, he pulled back. Barb felt his cock soften and immediately, his spunk flowed out and ran down the front of the machine. They could hear it hit the floor and she said, "Oops" and they both laughed.

He pulled her off and set her down away from the washer and Barb felt more of his seed run down her leg. She didn't bother to clean it up – there was just too much.

He grabbed some boxer shorts out of his basket and wiped down her leg. "Sorry about that," he grinned and they both laughed again. He moved to the washer to clean it as well.

Then the guilt began to set in.

"We shouldn't have done that," she said.

"Shhh," he said, straightening up. "Don't ruin it."

"But you said you wouldn't ruin my marriage vows," she responded.

He shrugged. "It was what you needed. Now you can say you now know what it's like to fu– uh, make love to a black man. It doesn't have to affect your marriage." He smiled. "It appeared you enjoyed it."

"God, it was…. it was…." She shook her head. "You should've worn a condom."

He had the decency to look chagrined. "I couldn't help myself. You were so sexy. But I'm clean, if that's what's worrying you." He paused. "I hope you…" he raised an eyebrow.

"Yeah. I'm on the pill."

"Good."

"Well, I'd better…" She turned to the machine and finished loading it. She could feel Carlos' eyes on her back. When she was done, she turned to face him. "This can never happen again."

He tipped his head. "If you say so." He moved to another machine and dumped his clothes inside.

Barb felt another rope of his spunk dribble down her leg and she suddenly wanted to go shower. "I'd better go."

"Come by my place anytime if you have an itch that your husband can't scratch," he said and winked.

Barb grabbed her empty basket and fled, her mind now free to feel guilty for what she had just done.

She returned to the apartment and immediately jumped into the shower. As she washed, she could feel Carlos' hands on her, the masculine smell of him, and his cock inside her, spreading her apart and reaching places that poor Dave never could. It just made her guilt worse.

"Never again," she pledged to herself, but she wondered if she could keep that promise.

Chapter Four

Barb was determined to rededicate herself to her marriage. What happened was a one-off – a mistake, sure, but something a sheltered white girl like her needed to get out of her system.

Okay, I've fucked a black man, she told herself. *I can chalk that off my bucket list. It's like visiting the Grand Canyon – I've seen it, now I can move on.* Then she giggled. *Only it wasn't the Grand Canyon – it was more like an Egyptian pyramid!*

She decided to seduce Dave that night as if to wipe out the memory of her infidelity. It didn't take much effort on her part. Dave seemed to be in the mood as well. Perhaps out of guilt, Barb didn't demand he use his tongue first. She told herself she was being extra nice to Dave, but she knew the real reason was she feared he might taste Carlos inside her and everything would be ruined. It was pleasant, the sharing, but ultimately unsatisfying, as always. She shouldn't have been surprised. What had really changed, after all?

When he squirted inside her and rolled off and began to snore softly, Barb fought back tears. *So much for forgetting all about Carlos's cock*, she thought.

She tried. She didn't want to run into Carlos in the hall and especially not in the laundry room. She began taking her clothes to the laundrymat down the block, feeling smug that she was being a good wife once again. *Avoid temptation.* She could hear her mother's voice in her head. Dave was a good man, he deserved a loyal wife.

A week went by, then another. Summer was fast approaching. She tried to work out her frustrations at the gym and it helped. The image of Carlos rutting with her in the laundry room began to fade, like a bad dream. She could almost pretend it didn't happen – almost. Yet every time she made love to Dave, it resurfaced. When Dave entered her, her pussy seemed to ask her, *Is that it? Are we doomed to go through life experiencing tiny Mr. Quick Squirt forever?*

Her cuckold fantasies began to return. She decided she needed to orgasm before she let Dave have his way and reinstated her demand that he bring her off with his tongue before he fucked her. He acquiesced, grudgingly, and she allowed herself to imagine what it might be like to cuckold Dave with Carlos. Would Dave be able to handle it? She doubted it, but maybe he was one of "those guys" who wanted to see his wife with another man. He had never said anything about it.

She didn't know how to broach the subject, however, and remained frustrated. Barb began reading more about it online and became careless with her search history. Maybe she was trying to get caught, she wasn't sure. But it didn't take long for Dave to find out what she was up to.

He didn't say anything to her, but she began to notice he'd taken an interest in using her laptop, telling her his was "on the fritz." She didn't think much of it until later, when she used it and found not only her cuckold sites in the history, but others too, ones she had never seen before. Some of them were so-called "sissy" sites, where men dressed up in feminine attire and got fucked by men with big cocks. The revelation shocked her. She decided to confront him.

"Dave, what's this all about?" she asked, showing him one of the sites in question.

He feigned ignorance. "What are you talking about? I don't know anything about it."

"Come on, don't lie to me. I didn't go to those sites!"

"But you went to other ones, almost like it!" he protested and she knew she had him.

"So you admit you've been looking, hmm?"

"Um, er... Hey, I was just using your laptop one night and found what you've been searching for. And yes, I admit I was curious. But you started it!"

She nodded. "I guess I did." She took a breath. "We should talk."

He grimaced. Those were the words no man wanted to hear.

"Things still aren't ... exactly right between us."

"What do you mean? We've been getting along better!"

"Yes, outside the bedroom. But I think you know it's not been ... uh, perfect there."

He rolled his eyes. "All that again?"

And other things, she thought. "I don't want to hurt your feelings..." she began.

He shook his head. "Fuck! You don't have to say it! I know! Fuck!" He stood up and walked out of the room and into the kitchen. Barb followed him.

"I'm sorry! But we have to talk about it!"

"I know, I know. I just don't like to hear it, you know? I can't do anything about it!"

"I'm sorry, honey – look, I love you. You're a good man, you have a good job, you'll be a great dad some day..." They had talked about starting a family when they were more settled.

"If I can get you pregnant, you mean! Me and my tiny penis. The one you can't feel!"

"I'm sure we'll have no trouble when the time comes!"

He shook his head. "I know. You want a guy with a bigger cock!"

"No! It's just a... fantasy, you know. I'm sure you look at ... some things. I mean, you were looking at some things that turned you on. Like maybe big boobs?" Barb had caught him more than once looking at women with big breasts and often teased him that her C-cups weren't enough for him. She wisely decided not to mention some of the other sites he had visited.

"I was just curious and following links here and there – I wasn't actively going to those sites like you've been every day!"

"It's only been recently," she said and realized she might've said too much.

"Why recently?"

"Uh… Just got in the mood, that's all."

Dave shook his head. "Come on, I know you better than that." He narrowed his eyes. "Most of those sites you visited were about black men. Don't think I'm stupid. This is about that neighbor, what's-his-name, isn't it?"

"Carlos," she said at once and knew no matter how she might deny it, she had just given herself away.

"I knew it!" He stared at her. "So what's going on? Should I be worried?"

"No! Nothing's going on!" *Except he kinda accidentally fucked me the other day and I want to do it again.*

"You've been fantasizing about him, haven't you?"

Somehow, this seemed better than the truth, so Barb pretended to be caught. "Uhhhh…."

"Fuck! I'll bet you're wondering how big his dick is, aren't you?"

"No! I mean… There are rumors about such things, but I don't know!"

"I'll bet you've seen it!"

Her face grew hot. "What?! Hell no!"

"I mean in his pants, silly. I've seen him walking around in his gym clothes half the time. I'll bet you passed him in the hall and he got a boner and you saw it bulging! Am I right?"

Whew! She was grateful he had given her an out.

"Uhhh... maybe." She stared at the floor.

"Fuck! I knew it! And ever since, you've found my little guy not worth the time!"

"No, it's not like that!"

"Look, I can't help the way I am. But you knew it when you married me. Now if you want to run off with some black guy, go for it. I won't hold you back!"

"I don't want to run off with Carlos! That's silly!" *I just want to borrow him now and then*, she thought and it shocked her.

"Yeah. I doubt he makes as much money as me."

"That doesn't matter. This isn't about money. I'm compatible with you – I love you. I hardly even know Carlos!"

"But you do know him, right? You've talked to him?"

"Sure, in the hallways," she said. "But I don't think he's my type." *Except for his cock. That was fucking perfect.*

"Okay, I get it now. It's all making perfect sense."

"What is? I'm not going to run off with Carlos, if that's what you're thinking!"

"Oh, no, I don't think that. I just think you'd like to have him come over now and then to fuck you, that's all."

Barb felt her heart beat faster and her face grew hot. She hesitated, not wanting to betray herself, but that pause made it all too obvious.

He nodded. "I shoulda known, the way you've been in bed and all. You want to cuckold me!"

Would that be so bad? "No!" She said. "No! I just... I just had a little fantasy! Can you blame me? I mean, lovemaking is usually about you, you know."

Dave had the decency to recognize his selfishness. "Hey, okay, I'm sorry about that. I know I'm, uh, kinda quick and all. I'll do better, I promise."

"That's what I was trying to do with those little games and such. I wanted to have fun too." She reached out and touched his arm. "And your tongue is quite talented."

He shrugged. "I guess."

"Look, I know this is a tough conversation to have, but I'm glad we can talk about it. That's what a marriage is all about, right?"

He nodded. "Right. You know I love you and I want you to be happy."

"And I feel the same. So we can work this out, okay?"

"Okay."

Chapter Five

Dave retreated to the bedroom, leaving Barb to clean up the kitchen. He should've helped, but he needed to get away and think. His overwhelming emotion was: *Whew! That was close!* How could he admit his cuckold fantasy to his wife without her thinking he was some kind of pervert? It was one thing to fantasize about it online, quite another to suggest they try it in real life!

The most embarrassing part to admit – even to himself – was how he got turned on by seeing shots of men in cock cages. And when they were made to wear panties and stockings by their "mistresses," well, he could guarantee a squirt, that was for sure! He had no idea why he liked it – he never considered himself to be a sissy or remotely homosexual. If he had to explain it, he'd confess it stemmed from his "inadequacy" between his legs. Growing up with a small penis tended to alter one's thinking about sex. If he couldn't satisfy a woman the regular way, he had to come up with alternatives – otherwise, they'd leave him – or worse, laugh at him.

Barb had never done that, of course. He'd been lucky to land her. Which is why it tore at him to try and find the balance between his ego and his fear. He'd do anything to keep her, he told himself, including giving better oral sex, although as a selfish male, he'd just as soon fuck her instead. It was this constant push-pull of his intellect versus his emotions that caused him to remain stuck, afraid to act out his fantasies for fear he might lose her and yet egocentric enough not to give her everything she wanted and needed for fear it would diminish him as a man. He had a perfect mess of emotions churning in his gut most of the time.

When someone like Carlos came along, Dave was torn between his desire to see Barb enjoy a bigger cock and his fear that she would leave him for someone like him. Probably not Carlos, but maybe the next guy or the one after that. Because that's what happened once a woman experienced a big black cock, he'd learned from his Internet searches – they can't go back to small white dicks.

* * *

A month went by, a month full of doubts and self-recriminations. June came warm and inviting, offering up its many possibilities. Barb remained true to her marriage, despite much temptation from the floor below. Carlos had sought her out more than once when he knew Dave was at work, but she had managed to keep him at bay, despite what her pussy was telling her.

"No," she told him just last week when he had come to her door. She had peeked out through the crack, refusing to open it wider. "I can't! I'm not that kind of woman!"

"Come on, I know you need it," he said in that low tone that made her pussy grow hot. "We don't have to tell Dave. Just sneak off to the laundry room now and then. Or, better yet, come over to my place."

"No! I'm trying to make my marriage work! What happened was a mistake!"

"But it was a pretty good mistake, you have to admit." He grinned at her and she blushed. "Listen, why don't you check to see if you have any clothes that need washing, hmm?"

"Please, Carlos! Go away!" She shut the door in his face and leaned against it. Whew! It had been a close call – her body fairly screamed at her to give in. She went into the bathroom and pulled her shorts down. Her pussy was dripping wet! A shiver went through her body as the memory of his hard black cock thrusting into her returned.

"Stop it," she begged. "Stop it."

Barb might've been able to handle Carlos better if her lovemaking with Dave had improved. But after his initial rash of promises, he had fallen back into his bad habits. She'd have to beg him to bring her off and half the time, he'd just climb on and take care of himself, leaving her frustrated. She wished she could exert more control over their sex life, but she didn't seem to have the right tools. Her earlier efforts just faded away. She wasn't the dominant type, she discovered. In fact, she preferred to be submissive, but she couldn't pull it off with Dave – he just wasn't man enough. She realized they were probably both submissive.

Her life seemed to be doomed to boredom until one Wednesday afternoon in late June, when she came home from work to find Carlos in the lobby, checking his mail – with another woman on his arm! She was a blonde floozy, with big breasts and ass in a tight dress. Barb felt an immediate rush of jealousy.

"Oh, hi, Barb!" he said casually. "How's it goin'?"

"Uh, fine."

He nodded and moved toward the elevator. He made no effort to introduce his girl to her. She watched out of the corner of her eye as they disappeared from view. She let a long breath out slowly and tried to get her emotions under control. Her reaction was totally inappropriate. So what if he has a girl? It was better for her anyway – now he won't be coming around pestering her, testing her will power.

I'm glad, she told herself. *Now I can stop being tempted!*

But the words rang hollow in her head. She decided to walk up, using exercise to blunt the image she had seen. She resisted the irrational urge to pause on the third floor and listen at their door. What was wrong with her? She shook herself and made it to the fourth floor without embarrassing herself. Barb let herself in and pressed her back against the door. She knew, without even thinking about it, that she would be spending some time with her fingers this afternoon.

The incident with the bimbo had a profound effect on her, one that she didn't want to admit to herself. The jealousy remained in her core, out of reach of logic. It was ridiculous, irrational and impossible, but it wouldn't go away. It would surface at all the wrong times, like when she was walking down the street and a handsome black man passed her. A sudden urge to feel Carlos' big cock inside her again would take hold and her vision would blur for a second. Then she'd shake her head and curse herself for her weakness and move on, determined to remain true to her husband.

True? The devil on her shoulder spoke up. *You haven't been true. You've already fucked him, what's one more time gonna hurt? Besides, you deserve it! You've been married too long to a guy who doesn't do it for you! Come on, live a little!*

Her angel responded: *You were practically assaulted!*

The devil sneered. *Oh, yeah, sure you were! So why didn't you report him? And why do you think about him all the time?*

Barb had no answer to that. Her pussy clenched and she knew her panties were sopping wet. Again. *Damn my life!*

Two days later, on Friday, she arrived home from work and once again found Carlos at the mailbox. He looked very handsome in his suit from work. This time, he was alone. Did he know when she usually came home? Did he time his own arrival to casually meet her? But her suspicions were swept away just by seeing him and she found herself speaking up before she could stop herself.

"Who was the girl?" she asked, and immediately her face went hot. "Uh… I mean… Sorry, that's none of my business."

"You mean Darlene?" he asked in that maddeningly calm

voice of his. "Why? You jealous?" He winked at her.

"Uh…" She decided it was useless to lie. "Maybe a little. She just looked… trashy."

"Sometimes a man likes trashy," he said and grinned. "But he likes classy too." He stepped closer and she lost her breath.

Barb wanted nothing more than for him to grab him in a tight embrace and kiss her. Take her arm and drag her up to his apartment and fuck the shit out of her. Her panties were soaked again.

He leaned down and whispered, "You can't fight it forever."

She found herself nodding. "But I'm married! I can't…"

"Sure you can. You just have to do one of two things," he said softly, "one, you can just come over once in a while when you're sure your husband won't know and scratch your itch. Or, you can level with him. Tell him that you need a big black cock now and then and he's just gonna have to be okay with it."

"No! He'd never do that!"

He nodded. "Sounds like No. 1 then…"

"No! I can't do that to Dave!"

Carlos shrugged. "So you're just going to go through life being frustrated?"

She sighed. "I guess."

"Sounds sad." He gathered his mail and moved toward the elevator. "Guess I underestimated you."

"Wait!" she said. "What does that mean?"

He turned. "It means I thought you were the type of woman who knows what she wants and goes after it. I didn't know you would be satisfied with so little."

"But… I don't want to hurt Dave."

"He might surprise you." He turned back toward the elevator.

Barb hurried after him. "Wait… What do you mean?"

"I mean, he might like to watch sometimes."

"Really? You think so? But ... I don't know... I mean... That's..."

"Speak up, girl! Forget Dave for a minute. Tell me what *you* want for once. Not the girl you think you should be, but the one that's hidden deep away, afraid to speak out. "

She stared at him, her body trembling. "I... I want to experience what I had before," she said. "But I feel so guilty about it."

He nodded. "Come on up. We'll talk."

She knew they would do a lot more than talk. Barb looked around, as if afraid someone might be watching. She turned back. "Just like that?"

"Just like that," he said and stepped into the elevator. "Up to you."

Barb hesitated until the door began to close in her face before reaching out and stopping it. The doors rolled back and she stepped inside with him, her conscience telling her this was a very bad idea. When they got to his floor, she hesitated. He turned and tipped his head at her and said nothing. She stepped out. At his door, she touched his arm. "You sure Darlene isn't in there, waiting for you?"

He flashed her a big smile. "No, you've got me all to yourself." He unlocked the door and stepped through. She followed, her stomach in knots.

Once she was inside, her doubts flared up anew. "I don't know about this." But her pussy had quite another viewpoint. She could feel her juices squishing in the gusset of her panties. *God*, she thought, *I wished I had trimmed up a bit down there!*

"I think you do," he said and closed the door behind her. She jumped. "Relax." He took off his suit coat and hung it on a peg by the door. He had on a pale blue shirt underneath and a tie that he had loosened.

"Sorry. I guess I'm nervous."

"Nothin' to be nervous about. You're in good hands." With that, he wrapped her in his arms and pulled her tight to him. It was exactly the right thing to do; it made her feel safe and comforted. Her anxiety eased for a moment.

"You have to wear a condom," she said and he gave her a level look.

"I didn't before."

"Yeah, but you should have! I don't know anything about you! You could have something – I might be infected right now!" *Like maybe from that floozy, Darlene.*

Carlos shook his head. "I told you. I'm clean."

"Still. We should've been more careful."

He nodded. "Sure. But soon, we'll want to dispense with those damn things."

Barb nodded. Now that she had set the ground rules, she felt more in control. Was she really going to do this? She guessed she was. Her pussy certainly wanted to!

She tried to push aside her guilty thoughts and tell herself that Carlos was right – she needed this! Dave won't have to find out. *What he doesn't know won't hurt me*, she thought as Carlos leaned down to kiss her.

"I'm a very bad wife," she told him.

"No you're not," he said, taking her hand and leading her to the bedroom. "You are just torn between what you *think* you should do and what you really need."

"I guess." It didn't make her a better person.

She didn't offer any further protest when he pulled her into the bedroom. Now she understood what men meant when they said they had been "thinking with their dicks." She was thinking with her pussy and it was quite damned demanding.

Carlos sat on the bed and maneuvered her between his knees. He leaned in and rubbed his face on her breasts and her nipples stood immediately at attention. Her pussy purred.

"I'm glad you're wearing a skirt today. I like you in skirts."

"I was at work," she said. "I have to dress up."

"Still, it's nice for me too."

She nodded, enjoying this bit of foreplay. She needed to go slower today and he seemed to know it.

His hands unbuttoned her blouse and she didn't stop him. Her bra came into view and he complimented her on it. She almost told him it was French and quite expensive, but stopped herself. He didn't care about that. "Thanks," she said simply.

He kissed her stomach as he pulled her tighter to him. She looked down to see the familiar bulge in his pants. It looked painful. No wonder why he wore sweatpants or shorts on the weekends.

"Does it hurt?"

He looked up, puzzled before the understanding hit him. "Why yes, these pants are a bit tight." He released his grip on her bottom and she stepped back. Her heart beat faster as he stood and unbuckled his pants. They fell to the floor and his magnificent cock tented his boxer shorts. He smiled as she stared and unfastened his tie and tossed it on the bed. Slowly, he unbuttoned his shirt and Barb wanted to tell him to hurry up. She fought her conscience again and kicked her angel right out of the room. She was tired of hearing her whiny little voice.

She needed this, damn it.

Carlos shucked off his shirt and tossed it aside. She expected him to reveal that wonderful cock but he sat down and untied his shoes and slipped them off and removed his pants. He folded them and went to hang them up.

Barb felt her body trembling. "Are you sure I should be doing this?" she asked him.

He smiled. "I'm sure. Think of it as medicine for what ails ya."

She nodded, her conscience quiet at last. Or maybe she was just kidding herself for the moment, so she could get laid without that scolding voice in her head.

He approached her and gave her a hug, running his hands over her back. She felt his fingers unfasten her bra and he stepped back, allowing it to fall down her arms. She shivered, but didn't stop him when his hands returned to her skirt. Soon it puddled down around her ankles, leaving her in her stockings and French panties, very sexy, which seemed appropriate. It made her feel that this was an elegant affair, not a sordid tryst.

He kissed her and she felt safe and warm in his embrace. He was so much stronger and bigger than Dave! It stirred a visceral feeling inside her, making her feel protected and yet entirely submissive. She could not stop what was happening now if she wanted to. All she could do was acquiesce to his power. It was very freeing.

Carlos bent down and picked her up easily in his arms. She gasped from the suddenness of it. He placed her gently on the bed and lay beside her. His fingers roamed over her body, making her pussy wetter by the second. Her body trembled.

"I wish I could make the guilt go away," she said.

"Just think of this as a spa day," he said.

She frowned. "A spa day?"

"Yeah. It's something you gals do for yourselves, right? You don't feel guilty about that."

"This is entirely different," she said dryly.

"Not if you think of it as something you do just for yourself, something you need to keep yourself sane."

Now it did make some sense, she decided. "A spa day… hmmm."

He grinned and kissed her again. She could smell the odor of her arousal and wondered if he knew how easy she was, how her body was betraying her. But Carlos seemed to be in no hurry, which was just what she needed. He seemed more attune to her body than even her husband was. He was powerful and gentle at the same time and Barb allowed herself to be seduced. It wasn't hard.

He bent down and took a nipple into his mouth and she moaned, low in her throat. Dave spent very little time on foreplay – a couple of quick kisses, maybe squeeze a breast and then get right to it. If it wasn't for her insistence that he give her oral sex, she doubted she would ever come again.

Carlos, on the other hand, knew what she needed instinctively. He was all man and yet sensitive and caring to her needs. When his hands moved down to her panties, she was ready. She raised her hips, telling him she wanted her panties gone and they soon slipped off her legs and he tossed them on the floor. She still had on her garter belt and stockings.

"You want me to take these off?" She waved a hand at her legs.

"No," he said. "It makes you more sexy."

She shivered. It was the right thing to say. She was offering herself up to him, her last vestiges of her modesty eliminated. She found herself spreading her legs even before his hands returned. It was a very clear signal: *I'm yours to take.*

Still he would not be hurried. He nibbled on her earlobe, he kissed the side of her neck, he took a nipple into his mouth, giving it a teasing bite. She groaned and her body felt aflame. She wanted to be fucked and tried to encourage him by moving her legs further apart as if to say, *I need your cock now.*

Carlos, to his credit, got the message. He moved over her, grasping her knees and moving her legs up to each side, opening her like a butterfly. Barb felt cool air on her wet pussy and knew she was more than ready for his thick cock.

Doubt suddenly gripped her. "Uh, I'm sorry – I should've trimmed up a little."

"You look beautiful. Now, enough talk…" He positioned himself over her.

When she felt the bulbous tip press against her, she suddenly remembered her promise to herself and gasped, "Condom!"

Carlos grimaced. "Fuck that," and pressed more of himself into her.

Held down like she was, Barb felt she could do nothing to stop him and she instantly gave up. It wasn't true, of course. She could have insisted. But she liked the helplessness of her situation, the feeling of a big, powerful man who had to have her and wouldn't take no for an answer. He wanted her bareback so she could feel his seed splash into her. It made her feel so desirable, her pussy fairly gushed, coating his thick cock with her juices.

More of his gorgeous cock slipped into her, making her mouth come open and her head tip back, as if it was too big and she had to make these adjustments to survive. "Oh! Oh my god!" she cried and felt her hips crack from the strain. His cock was almost all the way inside her and it was driving her crazy.

"You're so big!" she moaned. But he wasn't *too* big. In fact, he fit her perfectly.

Above her, Carlos grinned. He pulled back and gave her a moment's respite, then plunged back in, deeper this time. Again, her mouth came open and her head went back and she alternated between clinging to his arms and trying to push his big chest away. He wasn't about to stop and she felt his rhythm begin: In, making her eyes water and her pussy purr; out, giving her a break but leaving her pussy feeling desperately empty; then back in again, a little deeper, starting the process all over.

Carlos began to speed up his efforts and suddenly, Barb felt his balls slap her ass and realized he was all the way inside her now. His thick girth would stretch her out, leaving her useless to her husband and his four-inch dick. But the guilt would not return. She didn't give a damn about Dave at that moment, even if he was in the room, watching. In fact, the thought made her building orgasm increase in power and she cried out: "Yes! God yes! Fuck me! Fuck me in front of my husband!"

Carlos grinned and his fingers dug into the flesh behind her knees, forcing her legs up and apart even more, his hard cock splitting her, watching her head rock back and forth.

"Oh god! I'm gonna come! I'm gonna come!" she cried out, the sensation rolling up from her tightly curled toes through her thrumming pussy and rocking into her nipples before exploding in her brain.

"OH FUCK! OH FUCK! I'M COMING! I'M COMING!"

Carlos didn't break his rhythm. Barb couldn't come down from her orgasm before another one rolled over her, then another one. She was a rag doll, helpless to stop the pleasurable sensations that took control of her body and mind.

She felt his speed increase and opened her eyes to see his face in a grimace and said, "Yes! Yes, come inside me! I want to feel it!"

He bellowed and she could feel his cock throb deep within her. Another orgasm rocked her and she clung to him, her body throbbing in rhythm to his squirts.

At last their heartbeats slowed and Carlos rolled off of her and lay next to her, his hand still resting against her hip. Barb felt his seed gushing out and staining his sheets. She could not move. It was the best sex she had ever had. Again. She wondered why she hadn't dated a black guy earlier. Would she have married Dave if she had found a guy like Carlos five years ago?

"Wow," she said, her breath slowing.

"Yeah. Wow," He agreed.

Nothing more needed to be said.

Chapter Six

When she returned to her apartment, she felt wonderful. Her body purred, her pussy felt warm and tingly. The guilt she expected to feel wasn't there.

I needed this, she told herself. *Like a spa day*. She grinned. A moment later, she realized, *And I'll need it again.*

She took a long shower, washing away all evidence of her sins. As she was drying off, she caught her image in the foggy mirror. She stared at herself, guilt returning.

"So what do I tell Dave?" she mused aloud.

Could she continue to sneak around until she got caught? Or could she make Dave understand that she needed a good hard fucking now and then? Would he ever be open to such things?

She had to find out. Her angel had returned and she knew it wouldn't allow her to sneak around on her husband. She already knew Dave had some interest in looking at images of cuckolding couples online. He denied it, of course, but perhaps that was just because he had been caught. She needed to explore this further.

She got dressed and opened up Dave's laptop, something she hadn't bothered to do before. She searched his browser history. Sure enough, she found several sites devoted to cuckolding. She went to one of his favorite sites to explore.

By the time he arrived home forty minutes later, she decided to confront him and see what happened. Barb made no effort to conceal what she was doing when he walked into the bedroom and found her on the bed, watching a short film of a black man and a white woman in bed, the husband sitting on a chair nearby, his small dick in hand.

"What – what are you doing with my laptop?" Dave exclaimed.

"Just checking out your favorite website. It's pretty cool," she said nonchalantly.

"That's... I don't... Why are you doing that?" he sputtered.

"I was just curious. It *is* kinda exciting. I can see why you like it."

"Uh... I was just scrolling around, that's all," he said. "Shut it down – you shouldn't be looking at that!"

"Why not? You check it out all the time, according to your browser history." She turned down the volume, but let the images continue.

"That's.... that's none of your business!"

"We're married, so that makes it my business. What are you so afraid of? You worried I'm going to think you are a freak or something?"

He grimaced. "Well, yeah..."

"Don't worry, it's perfectly normal! Everybody has fetishes."

"Really? What's yours?"

She paused just long enough to tease him. "Ohh, I'd say this is right up there," she said, waving her hand at the screen.

"Really?" His face told her he wasn't sure how to process the information. "Is this about that new guy again?"

"I suppose. But it looks like you've been thinking about it too."

"Uh, no, not really." He looked away, his face turning pink.

"Oh, come on, Dave. I'm not mad or anything. Let's just talk, okay?"

He shrugged. "Nothing much to talk about."

"Okay, I'll talk. You promised you'd do better in the bedroom, but it's been hit or miss. I often go to sleep frustrated. So what are we going to do about it?"

He stared at the floor. "I dunno." He paused and added, "You want to go fuck that guy?"

"Carlos. His name is Carlos."

"Yeah, him? Is that what this is about?"

"It doesn't have to be him," she lied. "It could be someone else."

He just nodded, his lower lip caught in his teeth. "Like an affair, right?"

Barb paused to think through her next words. "No. An affair suggests that you wouldn't know about it. If it wanted to have one of those, would I be talking to you right now?"

He had to give a reluctant tip of his head to that.

"I'm talking about something else entirely. Something more like this," she said, pointing at the screen. On it, the husband was intently watching the big black man plow his wife while fondling his own cock.

"I... I... uh... I don't think I could do that."

"Why not? It certainly does excite you!"

"Th-that's j-just a fantasy."

"But you have to admit, our sex life hasn't been great. Don't you want me to be happy?"

He looked away. "I'd be afraid I'd lose you."

She got up off the bed and came to him. "Dave, I love you. Of all the men I dated, you came out on top. That means a lot to me. I don't want to lose you, either."

He looked relieved. "I guess I just was afraid, you know, because..." He shook his head.

"It's just one part of our marriage. And it's not your fault."

"I know, but it's hard to deal with when I can see that you're disappointed and all."

"So we fix it. And we let the rest of our marriage go on intact."

"You really think we could do that?"

"Yes! I don't want a divorce. I love only you! Okay?"

"So… does that mean what I think it means?"

"Only if you're okay with it."

Dave chewed on his lip again. "And if I'm not?"

"Then we go on without that part of it. I'm not going to sneak around behind your back." She felt bad lying, but it had to be done. She told herself it wasn't too late to stop her nascent affair.

"But if we did that, you'd resent it, right?"

"I didn't say that. But I would probably get frustrated, yeah."

He took a deep breath. "So, um, how would this work?"

"We'd find a guy that we both could agree on and invite him over. You'd be right there as well."

"You think we could find a guy like that?"

She couldn't believe her ears. Was he really going to go along with this? "I'm sure we could. But you have to agree and not get all jealous later."

"If I was there, I wouldn't be," he said and she could see the truthfulness in his eyes.

She nodded. "Okay. So let's start looking."

"Hell, I already know who you're thinking of."

Barb feigned ignorance. "Who?"

"That Carlos guy."

"Him? I don't really know him. He might be dangerous or something."

"I doubt it. I've seen him in his suit and tie. He works on Wall Street, doesn't he?"

She nodded. "I guess. Do you think he'd be interested?"

Dave smiled. "Who wouldn't be? But he'd have to agree

to the ground rules."

"And they are?"

He began counting them off on his fingers. "One, I have to be around whenever you two get together. Two, he has to wear condoms. Uh... Three, you can't fall in love with him and leave me."

She reached out and touched his face. "I told you: I would never leave you if I can get everything I want here."

"Yeah, you say that now."

"It's true. You're the man I want. I'm just talking about a dick here."

He nodded. "Good." He took in a breath. "Okay. So what's next? You call Carlos? Or are you gonna want me to do that?"

She smiled. That was unexpected. "You'd do that for me?"

He shrugged. "I guess. I mean, it might make the ground rules clearer, you know?"

Barb nodded. "Okay. But... I'm a little nervous about it. How would you approach him?"

"I dunno. I guess I'd just have to go down there and ask him some day." He made a face. "Like when would you want to do this?"

"Uhh... today's Tuesday, so ... maybe this weekend?" She wondered if her well-fucked pussy would recover by then. "I mean, if we're gonna do this, I think it should be soon or we'll just fall back into our old habits."

Dave nodded. "Okay. I'll talk to him. Jeez."

"Don't be that way about it! From what I understand on these websites, the husbands are all for it. It shows they really love their wives, but it also turns them on. Doesn't this turn you on?"

He looked away. "I guess. I just never thought you'd go for it."

"Well, you should've asked me sooner. We could've

cleared up a lot of misunderstandings."

"Uh huh."

When Dave left for work the next morning, she hurried down to Carlos' apartment, hoping to catch him before he had to go. When he opened the door, he was fully dressed in his suit. He face lit up when he saw her, making her body tingle.

"Hey there! Don't you look fine this morning! Sorry, I'm running late for work."

"I know – I just stopped by to give you the news."

He stopped, eyebrows up. "What news?"

"Dave agreed to let me take a lover." She grinned. "A black lover."

"Ohhh. Really? So he *is* one of those guys, huh?"

"Yeah. But the catch is – he wants to approach you, to go over the 'ground rules'." She made quotes in the air. "So act surprised. And don't let on that… you know."

"I'm not stupid! Don't worry, I'll handle it." He stepped out and closed the door and locked it. "So when is this gonna happen?"

"I don't know, but I suspect this weekend. You free?"

"Saturday, I am." He grinned. "So it looks like we're gonna get to have a lot more sex, huh?"

She blushed. "Stop it! You sound like a teen-ager. But fuck yeah, that's the idea."

He bent down and kissed her suddenly, catching her off guard. She felt the heat in her body increase. He pulled away and nodded. "Gotta go. See you this weekend!" He went off down the hall, whistling a happy tune.

* * *

Dave stood in front of Carlos's door Saturday morning and rocked from one foot to the other, his nervousness almost overwhelming him. How could he do this? Won't Carlos think him weird? Or worse, some kind of wimp? He guessed he was a wimp, considering what he was about to do. How did he let himself get talked into this?

Sure, the idea of watching his wife get fucked by a man with a big dick was one of the most secret of his guilty pleasures. When he looked at the videos, he could pretend it was him fucking those girls, making them come so hard they nearly passed out. The truth was, he'd known he had a small dick since freshman year in high school, when he had to shower with the other boys after gym class. No one pointed at him and laughed or anything – far too many of the other kids were in the same boat – but it was obvious that there were boys there who had big fucking dicks between their legs and from Dave's experience they were the biggest jerks. Unfortunately, they also got most of the girls.

The trend continued in college, much to his disappointment. By this age, most girls knew the range of dick sizes. For most, too big was too painful and too small wasn't worth bothering with. Dave's dates tended to go along fine until they got into the bedroom. They were rarely outright rude to him, but he'd notice their ardor would quickly cool and they'd start making excuses why they couldn't see him any more.

He was in grad school when he met Barb and he almost didn't go out with her, fearing it would turn out like all his other dates. Surprisingly, they hit it off. They both shared the same curious intellect, a wry sense of humor and life goals. After several dates, Barb hinted that she was ready to consummate their relationship and Dave had been terrified she'd leave him once she found out he didn't measure up.

When the fateful night came, she didn't run away screaming and actually seemed to enjoy herself. He had been so relieved, he asked her to marry him a week later. She told him it was too soon, but she liked the way he thought.

"Ask me again in six months," she told him. Those had been the best six months of his life. He had thought he was big enough for her and she seemed to enjoy herself. Only later did he find out she had been faking it.

To keep her interested, Dave had learned the fine art of

cunnilingus. Barb had really enjoyed it. True, over the years, he had allowed the practice to wane. Once he was married to Barb, he hoped his dick would be enough. He knew now he had just been selfish. He wondered if he had worked harder to pleasure her, would he be standing outside this man's door right now, gathering his courage to knock?

He had tried to put it off. He promised Barb that he'd do more to please her and gave her a pretty good orgasm two nights ago with his tongue. The sex afterward had been... challenging. He could hardly get enough friction going to get himself off and he had to use his fingers to help. His efforts did nothing to dissuade her from her position.

"Come on," she had told him. "You promised! This was supposed to be something we'd both enjoy, remember?"

He couldn't deny that the idea turned him on. The fantasy was one thing, but standing outside Carlos's door ready to ask him if he'd fuck his wife was something else! He and Barb had gone back and forth and he could tell she wasn't going to let this go, so he gave in – again. He wondered how Carlos was going to react. Would he sneer at him? Would he want to high-five him? Or maybe, just maybe, he'd tell him to get the hell away from him and go take his perversions somewhere else.

Dave took a deep breath and knocked on the door.

I hope he isn't home! He thought. At that moment, the door opened and he was staring up at the handsome black man. Today Carlos was dressed in a Michael Jordan T-shirt and basketball shorts.

"Uh, hi," he said lamely, bracing himself for the ordeal ahead.

"Hi!" Carlos said brightly. He seemed genuinely glad to see him. "It's Dave, right? From upstairs? I hope I haven't been making too much noise!"

"Oh, no, not at all!" he said, feeling relief wash over him for a brief moment. At least he seemed nice. "Uh, I... Uh..."

The nervousness returned as soon as tried to figure out a way to explain his presence.

"Come in, come in," Carlos said, stepping back. "Want a cup of coffee?"

"Uh, yeah, thanks." He went in and looked around. The apartment was small, like theirs, but neatly kept. He didn't know what he had expected – maybe some old pizza boxes and a big-screen TV blaring a basketball game?

Carlos poured them both mugs of coffee and handed one to Dave. "Here, sit." He pointed to the small couch and followed him into the living room. Dave sat on the couch, cup in hand, trying not to bite his lip. Carlos took an upholstered chair oppose the small coffee table.

"What's on your mind?"

"Uhhhhh…."

Jeez, Dave thought. *How can I explain that my wife wants you to fuck her – that she isn't getting what she needs at home?* It was probably the most embarrassing thing a man could admit. "Well, it's kinda embarrassing."

"Don't be embarrassed. We're just a couple of guys here talking."

"That's part of it. I mean, it's not like we know each other all that well. I mean, we've hardly talked in the hallway or anything."

"So let's be friends. I don't want to move into this building and not know my neighbors and consider them friends. I mean, at least a few of them."

Dave nodded, relieved. "Well, that's good. It's just that, well, you know… I wasn't sure if you'd want to be friends."

"You mean, the black and white thing?"

Dave nodded. "Yeah. Sometimes you guys aren't exactly friendly."

"Well, I hope I'm different. Hell, I work on Wall Street! That's pretty mainstream. I'm not selling drugs or anything."

"Oh, no, no! I didn't mean that. I just meant, you know,

sometimes you guys can seem intimidating at times, that's all."

"I'm just a regular guy who happens to be black. So let's let all that racial stuff slip away, okay?"

Dave nodded again. He took a sip of his coffee. "Um, well, that's why I'm here, actually. The racial stuff."

Carlos frowned. "What do you mean?" His voice changed, as if he was ready to be insulted and was on his guard.

"Black guys … Uh… they often are bigger, right? Er, you know? Uh, I mean, isn't that what the ladies say?" He felt like an idiot for dancing around the subject, like some kind of delicate flower who was afraid to say the word "cock."

Carlos nodded slowly, a sly grin tugging at the corner of his mouth. "Yeah, I guess that's true. Not in all cases, but generally, yeah."

"My wife thinks you're one of the, um, more well endowed ones. Is that true?"

"Where exactly is this going?" His tone was neutral, but wary.

"Uh… It's about my wife. Barb. You've talked to her, right?"

"In passing. She seems like a real nice lady."

"Yeah. She is. But, uh…"

Carlos took a sip of coffee and waited.

"It's really embarrassing…" Dave wasn't sure he could get the words out.

"Are you trying to tell me Barb wants to experience a black man?" Carlos offered.

Dave nodded. "Yeah." He felt relieved now that it was out in the open. "I know it sounds crazy, but–"

"Not at all! I've seen this before."

That caught Dave up short. "You have?"

"Sure. I think it's on every white woman's bucket list. You know, to try a BBC at least once in their lives."

Dave nodded. From his Internet explorations into the subject, he knew what BBC meant: Big Black Cock. "So that's why I'm here. Uh, Barb wants to explore a little and we wondered if you'd…"

He grinned. "Sure!"

"Really? Just like that?"

"Only if you're okay with it."

"Well, that's why I'm here – to go over the ground rules."

Carlos nodded. "Sure." He sat back, coffee mug in hand. "Shoot."

"Well, first of all, this is just a temporary thing. I mean, I don't want you guys falling in love and taking her away or anything."

"I'm not ready to settle down, so you're okay on that front. 'Sides, I barely know your wife."

Dave nodded. "Second, you'd have to wear condoms. I mean, that's important."

"Are you worried about diseases and such?"

"Yeah, plus…"

"What? You don't want my bodily fluids contaminating your wife? I can tell you I don't have any diseases."

"It's not like that. It's more like… it's not cheating if you're not completely touching. Maybe that sounds crazy…"

"A little, maybe." He grinned. "But they're your rules. Anything else?"

"Yeah. I have to be there."

"Ohh, one of those guys, hmm?"

Dave felt his face grow hot. "Don't make it sound like that!"

"Sorry. But it does explain things, doesn't it?"

Dave shrugged. "I guess." He took a deep breath. "So, what do you think? Are you interested?"

Carlos leaned forward, put his mug down on the coffee table and rested his forearms on his knees. "Sure. When do you want to begin?"

Chapter Seven

"You really asked him?" Barb was incredulous. "You went down there and asked him?" She had expected he'd back out and leave the job to her. It would have been far easier. More along the lines of: "Hey, Carlos, Dave said he's all for it – so when can you fuck me again?" They would've shared a big laugh and that would have been that.

"Yeah, sure. I mean, that's what you wanted, wasn't it?"

"Sure... but... that must've taken guts."

Dave bristled. "You don't think I have guts?"

"Not at all! I'm just surprised that you did it so quickly and all."

"It wasn't easy – I'll admit that. But Carlos seems like a nice guy. Better him than some thug."

"I'm not really into thugs, dear," she told him, fighting back the shiver whenever she thought of the way Carlos took possession of her body. *Like a thug in a suit*, she thought.

"I'm not really sure what you look for in a man. I mean, you know, in that arena."

"Sooo," she said, moving on. "What's next?"

"That's up to you, I guess. When do you want to do this?"

"Gee, I don't know," she said, trying to ignore the heat she felt rising from her pussy and spreading into her stomach. "Maybe next weekend?"

Dave pursed his lips. "Really? You'd want to wait another week?"

His attitude surprised her. "You want me to do it sooner?"

"Well, Carlos did mention that he was free tonight, so...."

"Tonight!" So soon? It wasn't that she didn't want to fuck Carlos again, she realized – it was that she wasn't exactly happy about having Dave watch the two of them together.

"Well, if you're not ready…"

"No, no – I can do this… Um… what will you be doing while we're, you know, doing it?"

"I'll be there. I can sit in this chair in the corner. Won't that be okay?"

"I don't know. It might be kinda weird, having you watch us."

"Why? I mean, isn't that why we agreed to all of this? I'm not having you sneak around, if that's what you mean."

"I don't want to sneak around!" she lied. "It's just a bit strange, that's all."

"We can forget the whole thing if you'd rather."

"No," Barb said at once. "Let's call him."

"You call him. I'm kinda out of things to say to him."

"Really?"

"Sure."

"You get his phone number?"

Dave smiled and handed her his phone. "Ohh, you've got it right in there already," she noted. She dialed, her nerves jangling.

"Hello? Carlos, it's me, Barb."

"Hey, baby," she heard in her ear. She smiled nervously at her husband. "Uh, Dave said he talked to you and …"

"Anytime, baby. I can't wait to see you again."

"He said you were free tonight? Is that right?"

"Ohh, he must be right there, huh?"

"Yes, that's right." Barb gave Dave a nervous smile.

"Tonight will be fine. You want to come to my place?"

"No, let's have you come up here. I think we'll be more comfortable."

"Sounds good to me. Say seven?"

"That sounds good. Um… do you have, uh, condoms?"

"Yes, I do – but I hate the damn things. I hope that part of the rules will change."

"Me too," she told him. "See you then."

She hung up and smiled at Dave. "It's all set."

"Wow. I can't believe we're really gonna do this."

"Neither can I." She looked around. "My god! I've got to clean up this place! Come on, you can help!"

* * *

At seven, the knock came, startling both Dave and Barb. They had been expecting it, but they still jumped at the sound. They looked at each other as if to say: *Sure you want to do this?*

Barb certainly did. Her pussy throbbed at the thought of Carlos's big cock – only this time, it would be above board, sanctioned by her husband. She had taken a long time to prepare herself for this night. She had showered and trimmed up her bush and applied perfume and just the right touch of makeup. She had selected four different outfits before deciding on a sexy skirt and blouse, but she skipped the stockings. Too much, she had decided. She was as ready as she'd ever be.

She jumped up and opened the door.

"Hi," Carlos said.

Barb's knees grew weak. "Uh, hi. Come in."

Carlos entered and spotted Dave sitting on the couch. Her husband rose to greet him. "Hi." He didn't offer his hand, he just waved. Carlos nodded and said, "Hey."

It appeared to be the start of a very awkward evening.

"Wanna a drink?" Dave asked him.

"Sure."

"Beer okay?"

"That'll be fine."

Dave headed to the kitchen. Carlos turned to look at Barb and smiled. She gave him a nervous smile in return and shrugged her shoulders as if to say, *Not sure how I feel about all this.* Carlos reached out and touched her shoulder, making her feel a bit less nervous.

Dave returned with two beers and handed one to Carlos.

"What about me?" Barb asked.

"Sorry – I ran out of hands. What would you like?"

"Glass of wine."

He nodded and returned to the kitchen. Carlos took the opportunity to bend down and kiss Barb on the cheek. She gasped and looked guiltily toward the kitchen, as if she was afraid Dave might catch them. She realized how silly that was and laughed at herself. *It's not as if there won't be kissing!* she told herself.

Dave gave her the wine and they all sat, Dave and Barb on the couch and Carlos opposite. They sipped their drinks in silence. Finally Dave spoke up: "Soooo, here we are."

"Here we are," Carlos agreed.

Silence.

"Um, how should this all work?" Barb piped up. "I mean, I know this is awkward. How do we break the ice?"

"We could get drunk," Dave suggested.

Carlos shook his head. "No, not for me. I'll just have a beer or two. I like to stay clear-headed." He smiled at Barb. "I think the best way to begin is for Dave and me to switch places."

Dave nodded but he didn't move at first. He seemed frozen.

"Change your mind?" Carlos asked him.

"No, no," he said, suddenly getting up. "I'm just nervous, I guess."

"Yes, I'm sure we're all a bit nervous." Carlos took Dave's place and sat down next to Barb. He turned toward her and smiled. Dave seemed to retreat into the background.

"Have you done this before?" asked Barb. She took a sip of wine.

Carlos tipped his head. "A few times."

Her eyebrows went up. "Really?" She knew about Darlene, she just didn't know there were other married women.

He nodded.

"So what was it like? Where they all married? Where they white girls?" The questions tumbled out of her. This time, she took a big gulp of wine to hide her jealousy and embarrassment.

Carlos smiled. "Yes, they were all white – and married. They felt the same way you guys do, I suppose."

"Are... are you still seeing them?"

Carlos tipped his head. "Just one. She's what you might call a regular."

Barb felt a sudden, irrational pang of jealousy. "So you make a habit of this? Servicing married women who want to experience... you know." Another sip. The wine was almost gone now.

"I wouldn't call it a habit, no. I don't go out searching for married women if that's what you mean. I just happen to fall into opportunities, like this one."

Barb nodded, realizing they had done more to create this situation that Carlos did. He probably would've been happy to fuck her behind Dave's back once in a while. By having Dave involved, it brought it more out into the open and made it seem almost mundane.

"I'm not sure how I feel about you fucking another married woman," she said.

Carlos glanced toward Dave. "I'll bet Dave is not sure how he feels about you fucking another guy, right?"

"Yeah," Dave agreed. "Maybe you don't wanna do this."

"No," she said at once. "I mean, we're all here and all..." She shook her head. "I'm sorry – I'm just ... I don't know...

nervous or something."

Carlos reached out and cupped his hand against her cheek. "I know. It's a big step. But you wanted this, right?"

She nodded. Carlos turned to Dave. "It's not too late to call it off, if you want."

Dave took a slow, deep breath. "No," he finally said. "I want Barb to be happy. If this makes her happy, I'm behind it."

Carlos nodded. "Then let's get started." He brought his fingers underneath Barb's chin and turned her face toward his and bent down to kiss her gently on the lips.

"Ohh," he said, "that's nice."

Barb felt very self-conscious. She kept stealing glances over at Dave, worried he would be upset. What man wouldn't be? Sure, she knew he liked to check out websites that features such things, but to sit there and watch another man fondle his wife was quite something else. And a black man besides. Put aside the racial aspect of it, Barb was far more worried about what Dave would think when Carlos pulled his dick out! Would he feel even more inadequate? Would he want to call it off? And what if he did? Would Carlos stop, mid-fuck, so to speak? Barb doubted he could be stopped, once he got going. She already knew how strong and overpowering he was.

All this talk made it very hard to relax and get into the moment. She felt stiff and, well, unsexy. Carlos noticed right away.

"Hey, relax. We're all here to have fun." He turned to Dave. "I think your wife needs another glass of wine."

Dave, to his credit, jumped up at once and refilled her glass. She took a grateful sip. When she returned her attention to Carlos, her body felt a bit more languid, which helped, but knowing Dave was sitting there still had a negative effect on her. After a few more gentle kisses, she broke away.

"I don't know about this," she said. "I'm just so jumpy!

I feel I'm being judged, even though Dave is being a perfect gentleman. Sorry, honey. I'm just all wound up."

"It's okay, Barb – I'm not upset or anything. I'm just sitting here."

"I have a suggestion," Carlos put in. Both Dave and Barb turned toward him. "Why don't we go into the bedroom for, say, fifteen minutes. Then you come in, quietly, and sit in the corner. That will give Barb a chance to relax. Okay?"

Dave nodded. "I can agree to that. Okay with you, honey?"

Barb felt a wave of relief. "Oh yes! Sure!" She hoped she didn't sound too eager.

Carlos stood and helped her up.

"Um, so should I set the timer or something?" Dave asked.

Barb laughed. "Just use your watch – I think having the timer go off might distract us."

"Oh, right! Sure."

She could tell he was nervous too.

"Just don't start without me. I mean, you know, too much."

Carlos gave Barb a knowing look and she fought a smile. "We won't," she said. "Just be quiet when you come in, don't break the mood."

He nodded and Carlos led Barb down the hall. Once inside the bedroom, Carlos looked around. "Nice," he said.

"Fuck that, let's get started before he gets in," she whispered. "God! I was *sooo* tense having him watch us! I felt like a cheating wife!"

Carlos laughed and began stripping Barb out of her clothes.

"Wait – are we just gonna strip down so quick like that?"

"Didn't you just say…" Carlos stopped and shook his head. "Never mind." He leaned down and gave her a long hug, followed by a slow kiss. "Better?"

She nodded. "Much. Sorry – I'm kind of a mess, I know."

"It's just because it's new. You'll get used to it."

"Do you think so? I'm not sure I can have Dave watching all the time."

"He doesn't have to. You can come up to my place anytime."

"Yeah, but that's kind of the point. It's not cheating if he's watching, right?"

He tipped his head. "I guess. I'm just thinking of what you're trying to get out of this. I mean, besides some good sex." He slipped off her blouse and kissed a bare shoulder. She shivered.

"I think that's all I'm looking for. Don't you?"

"It depends on your relationship with your husband. Some wives like to take the opportunity to really cuckold their husbands, if you follow me."

Barb had read up about it, but wasn't sure she was that kind of wife. "I think I'd have to be more dominant than I am to pull that off," she told him. She was down to her bra and panties now and felt suddenly exposed and helpless. Carlos was still fully dressed.

At that moment, she realized this is what she craved – being subservient. She loved being treated like a sexual plaything to a powerful man. Her nascent affair with Carlos brought up all those old feelings, the ones she had repressed when she married Dave, the safe choice.

Sometimes, safe was boring.

"This is what I like," she said, as Carlos eased her bra off her shoulders. "This feeling of being at the mercy of a man who just has to have me."

He nodded. "It's common, especially for accomplished women like you."

That pleased her. "So I'm not a freak?"

"Hell no. It just means you need to be submissive once in a while."

She nodded. "I guess so."

"And Dave can't do that." He bent down and slipped her panties down her legs. She shivered.

"No, he can't. He's not the type."

"And I think the big dick helps."

She laughed and felt more relaxed.

Carlos stood tall. "Now. Enough talk." He kissed her again, his hands rubbing her back, drifting down to her pear-shaped bottom and giving it a squeeze. Barb felt herself getting wet for the first time that evening. Usually Carlos's presence was enough to start the pussy to weeping, but tonight had been quite different.

He reached down and tossed the bed covers off. "Get into bed," he said in that deep voice of his and she quickly obeyed. She watched as he stripped off his clothes and climbed in next to her. They lay on top of the sheets, arms and legs intertwined. They kissed and groped and explored each other's bodies as if for the first time. Carlos seemed to know to go slow and let Barb get on top so she could control the pace of their lovemaking. As much as Barb wanted him, she would feel guilty if they were already fucking when Dave walked in. Like any good wife, she wanted to share.

* * *

When the door opened a few minutes later, Barb didn't notice at first, but Carlos did. He paid no attention as Dave slipped in and sat in a chair in the corner of the room. Instead, he rolled Barb over until she was on the bottom. Remembering their conversation, Carlos didn't want Barb to have control, so she could tell Dave she was helpless to stop him. And she was. Carlos took his time getting his cock into her. He got up on his knees so Dave could see the thick cock he had between his legs. He thought he heard a small gasp from Dave and it made him harder. He rubbed the shaft against Barb's very wet pussy and smeared the juices over her fuzzy mound. He knew he'd be asking her to shave that someday soon, if this little adventure continued. He just liked his women to be smooth.

When she was squirming and practically begging for it, he eased the tip into her and watched her mouth come open and her head start to tip back, as if he was too big for her. He liked it.

"Condom!" He heard from Dave and thought: *Shit!*

"Sorry, man," he said and pulled away. Barb looked like she'd just had her puppy stolen, but she didn't say anything. She just watched as Carlos found a condom in his pants pocket and tore open the wrapper. He slipped it on and felt both sets of eyes on him. His cock began to wilt and he climbed back over Barb quickly to regain the momentum that Dave had interrupted. He kissed her fully erect nipples and that helped his cock return to its full strength.

Her legs came up and apart to better ease the passage of his cock into her. She no longer seemed to care about her husband's presence. Carlos had seen it before – right now, all she thought about was big black cock.

He pulled back and fed more of his cock into her. By now, their third time fucking, she had already been stretched out and his member slid in more easily. Barb gasped and said, "Ohhh, you're sooo big!"

Carlos wondered how that was playing with Dave, but didn't bother to check. He began moving, sliding more and more of his cock into her until he felt his balls slap against her ass. She was making all kinds of noises now. Carlos smiled. He doubted she ever made those noises with Dave, at least from his experience with the other wives.

He took his time, bringing Barb to three separate orgasms, by his count. There may have been more. They way she writhed underneath him, her mouth wide open, her head tossed back and forth, it could have been more. Or maybe it was just one big orgasm. Carlos sped up and Barb's hands fluttered about, alternating between grabbing his arms and pushing against his chest, as if to stop him. He would not be stopped. His cock thrust hard against her, going deep and stirring his own release. He grimaced and his seed was suddenly launched into her, blocked only by the condom. He grunted and felt his cock throb and throb again, releasing the endorphins in his brain that made everything better.

He sank down, using his elbows to keep from crushing the small woman underneath him. His cock softened and he pulled out. Looking down, he could see the tip of the condom was full of his cum and again he regretted the need for the damn thing. *Soon*, he thought.

He rolled off the bed and went out the door and into the bathroom across the hall. He tossed the condom into the garbage and returned. He was curious to see how Dave felt about the experience.

When he walked in, neither one was talking. Barb had pressed herself up against the headboard, two pillows supporting her head, staring at Dave. He was sitting up in his chair. Carlos could see the small bulge in his pants, but noted he had not tried to free it for a quick wank while they were busy. He was chewing on his lower lip, as if he hadn't decided how he felt about it all.

"Well?" Carlos asked, breaking the tableau. Both pairs of eyes swiveled to the naked black man standing there. "Are you both okay?"

Barb waited, her eyes on Dave. When Dave finally nodded, she nodded as well.

"Yeah, fine," Dave said. "I'm fine."

He didn't sound fine. Seemed like a good time to leave the two of them to talk. "Well, I'd better go," Carlos said, pulling on his clothes. No one spoke again. "Call me if you'd like to see me again."

Barb just nodded, her eyes darting from Carlos to Dave.

"Uh, uh," Dave said. Carlos left, wondering if this marriage was about to explode.

Chapter Eight

After Carlos left, silence descended upon the room. They locked eyes, as if daring the other to speak first.

"Well," Barb said at last. "Are you upset? Do you want a divorce?"

"No, no," Dave said at once. "It was just … kinda… I don't know."

"What? Talk to me!"

"I guess up until this moment, I just hadn't realized just how much you needed a big, uh, penis. I mean… it was pretty obvious."

Barb blushed. "Don't make me feel self-conscious."

"I'm not trying to! I'm just giving you my impression, that's all. I mean, it was clear that you enjoyed that – way more than you ever enjoyed making love to me."

His voice was wistful and Barb hurried to reassure him. "No, that's just one part of it! You're the man I love – and the man I married. You're everything I want in a man!"

"Except for one very important part."

A wave passed over her face. She couldn't deny it. "Yes, well… I guess that's why we conducted this little experiment, huh?"

"Yeah, and I'd have to say the experiment was a resounding success. The next question is, What do we do now?"

"What do you mean?" She knew exactly what he meant, but she wanted him to spell it out.

"I feel like there's no point in us making love any more. Whenever you're in the mood, you just call Carlos over and..." He trailed off.

"It's not like that! I love our ... alone time."

"Sure, the cuddling maybe. Maybe even sleeping together. But if you need to get your rocks off, so to speak, it's obvious what you need."

"Was I that... wild?" She felt embarrassed to let Dave see that side of her. She would have preferred to keep it between her and Carlos.

"Don't get me wrong. I'm not mad or anything. In fact, I was happy for you. I mean, that's what love is, right? You want your partner to be happy."

She nodded. "But not at the expense of the other!"

"That's what I'm wrestling with, I guess. If you are to be happy, that means I don't get to have sex for the rest of my life."

"No! Of course you do! You can still make love to me!" She wondered if he would want to make love to her right now. Sometimes husbands like that – sloppy seconds. "Come on, come here!"

Dave didn't move. "Wait. I need to talk this out first."

Barb bit her lip. "Okay. I don't want to hurt you."

"No, actually, it was ... quite an education, watching you two. I'm just not sure how I feel about it."

"Didn't it ... turn you on a little?"

"Sure. Sure it did. I wanted to ... you know... take care of myself while you guys were going at it, but..." He shrugged. "I guess I felt ... inadequate."

Barb almost said something reassuring, but knew it would be a lie, so she didn't speak.

"I know it's not your fault. It's just... startling to see what I'm up against."

"We don't ever have to do it again if it makes you feel this way."

"I'm not sure I want that. Because I know that you'd go around pining for a big dick like Carlos's and that means one day, you'll start sneaking around. I don't want that. So I'm just trying to wrap my head around all this, you know?"

"I guess. But I'm willing to do whatever you want. I mean, we followed your rules tonight, didn't we?"

"Yes, we did. I think what is affecting me is just how good you two were together. I wouldn't have expected that from your first time together."

Barb felt a rush of blood to her face and tried to cover up her guilt. "I guess he was just a good fit."

"That's my point. I'm not. And I never will be." He got up and started out.

"Wait! Where are you going?"

"I need another drink."

Barb hurriedly slipped into her robe and followed him out. He was sitting on the couch, sipping a splash of bourbon in a short glass. He barely looked up when she entered.

"I could use one of those too," she said.

He nodded absently and jerked his head toward the bar. "Help yourself."

She poured herself a shot and sat on the chair facing him. "We have to talk, David. I feel like I've let you down or something."

"No, no. You're good. It's just ... I guess I was fooling myself."

"No! You're a good lover... I just couldn't always come, that's all!" She tried to make it sound like a little thing.

"I think that's the whole point. No, it's not you, Barb, and I don't want you to feel guilty. I'm just trying to figure out what to do next."

"This doesn't sound at all like your fantasies."

He gave her a half-grin. "I guess not." He paused. "Well,

in a way, maybe they were."

"How do you mean?"

"I mean, I would love to be a guy like Carlos, to make a woman come like that. Since I'm not, I guess I've been living vicariously through those websites and videos. You know, pretending not to be the cuckold, but to be... I don't know... the bull. It's a fantasy, sure, but I've been on the wrong side of it."

"It's understandable." Barb took a sip. "Well, we're never doing that again!"

"No, that's not the answer. I just have to get my mind right."

"You don't have to! I love you the way you are."

"Just let me think, okay? I can't rush this."

"Sure."

* * *

Barb went to bed early, leaving Dave alone to think. He still felt stunned by what he had seen and wanted to sort it out in his head. They clearly had a great connection, Carlos and Barb. He hadn't expected that. Part of him had hoped that Carlos would be too much for his wife to handle and she'd come running back to him. But another part had really enjoyed the show, to the point where he wanted to rub himself to a climax at the same time they did. He had been too embarrassed, although he could see it happening later, when he was more used to seeing the two of them together.

And that was the crux of his dilemma. Did he want to see the two of them again or did he want to call it off? He imagined he could convince Barb not to see Carlos again, but to what end? She'd resent him and pine for a cock like the one Carlos wielded. No doubt, sometime in the future, they'd be right back here again, only with someone named Leon or Bubba. No, Carlos was the devil he knew and if he had to pick a man for Barb, it would probably be a guy like him. He was educated, intelligent and sensitive. Under different circumstances, he might even like the guy.

He poured himself another short bourbon and sipped it as he tried to decide what he should do. He had to admit to his secret self that it was probably the most erotic thing he had seen in his life. Much better than the videos he'd been watching online. This was in 3-D! With Smell-O-Vision! He had wanted to join them, to lie next to Barb and watch as Carlos fucked her. Maybe even kiss one of her nipples or, more intimately, lick her pussy while… He shivered.

God, he thought – *that's what's bothering me! I really liked it but my ego says I shouldn't have. I wanted to be the only man in Barb's life, to be able to satisfy her like those boys in the schools he had attended had satisfied their girls.*

He had to let go of that now. In some ways, it was freeing. He could explore that dark side of him that he had kept hidden, the one that looked up cuckold videos or sissy videos and masturbated to the images, only to feel a little ashamed afterward. He had fought it and had trouble admitting to himself that the images excited him. Truth was, he was already a cuckold – he had given his permission and he had watched! He was too far down the rabbit hole to turn back now.

Dave got up and retrieved his laptop. He hoped Barb was already asleep. He didn't want to be caught looking at porn, not tonight. He sat on the couch and found one of his favorite videos, one that showed a cuckold man being shamed and taunted by his wife and her bull. He couldn't explain why it excited him, he just knew that if he wanted a quick squirt, this was his old stand-by. He ran the video, with the sound almost all the way down and watched, his hands already reaching for his zipper.

The bull – in this case, a white man – and the wife made the husband strip before they'd let him watch and Dave could see the steel cage he had between his legs. His own cock stood up in his underwear and he quickly freed it. He wondered what it would be like to wear one. He would never, not in a million years, buy one for himself. But if Barb or Carlos forced him, he could see it happening. He'd protest, no doubt, but deep down, he was curious to see what it would be like. The helplessness, the submission. It would drive him wild and torment him at the same time.

The wife took the bull's cock into her mouth, the naked cuckold lying on the bed next to them. The wife turned and said something Dave couldn't hear, but he had heard it enough times before to know she was telling him how big the man's cock was and how much better it felt. The husband looked ashamed and he tugged at his caged cock. The wife mocked him and said he wouldn't be freed for at least a month, depending on how well he cleaned them up afterward.

Dave's cock was fully erect now and he began to rub it, his eyes locked onto the screen. The wife laid down and spread her legs, inviting her bull to fuck her. The man loomed over her and eased his big cock into her pussy, while the husband bit his lip and looked pained. Dave knew they were hamming it up for the camera, but he didn't care. He had felt very much like that just a short time ago.

The couple were fucking in earnest now and Dave tried to time his stroking with theirs, so he wouldn't come too soon. He really liked the ending. The wife had her legs locked around her lover's thighs and was saying all sorts of nasty things. Dave didn't need the sound up for this part. The video spooled out and the bull neared his climax. Dave still didn't come – he knew what was coming next. The man stiffened and erupted into the woman and Dave was close now, he just had to hang on for a bit more…

When the man pulled out, the camera zoomed in on the white fluid as it started to leak out. The wife spoke sharply to the husband and the poor man rolled over and began licking up the discharge.

"Oh god!" Dave whispered and came all over his hand.

* * *

Barb thought Dave might need a day or two, but a week

went by without further discussion of their new situation. Whenever she tried to bring it up, he'd just shake his head and say, "Not yet."

She decided to talk to Carlos about it, to see if he had insights, based upon his experience with other wives. She knocked on his door several days later when Dave was still at work and felt her pussy throb when he opened the door. He had just gotten home and was still dressed in his suit, although he had ditched the coat. His face lit up.

"Barb! Long time no see! You come by for a visit?"

She knew what he meant by the term "visit."

"No," she said. "We need to talk."

He nodded and opened the door wider. "Come in. I was just about to change into something comfortable."

"Please... don't. Not yet." She didn't trust herself if he put on his sweatpants and his bulge would be obvious. Not that it wouldn't be obvious in his slacks, but someone, the formality of his clothes helped cool her ardor.

He nodded and waved her to a chair and sat down across from her. "Shoot."

Barb sat. She wasn't sure how to start.

"Would you like something to drink?"

Yes, she thought. "Um, wine, if you have it? If not, whiskey... or bourbon."

He nodded and jumped up to fix them both a drink. "Ice?" he said, pouring them both a shot of bourbon.

She shook her head and he returned with two short glasses with generous splashes of the amber liquid and she took a grateful sip. The smooth alcohol warmed her throat.

She took a deep breath. "Okay. I think Dave kinda freaked out."

"How so?"

"Well, he went on about how inadequate he felt now and how it was obvious that I needed a big cock and he said he needed time to think. And since then, nothing."

"It's only been a week. Give him time."

"Yeah, but it doesn't sound good, does it? I'm afraid we really hurt him."

"Maybe he's just coming to grips with the new reality."

"I think he's afraid I'll leave him."

"Really? Does he think we have that kind of relationship?"

"I guess he thinks where the cock goes, the pussy will follow."

Carlos laughed. "Is that how you see it?"

"No! I know you're just a fling! Besides, you have other women to occupy your time." She tried hard not to sound jealous.

"Yeah, so why is he so worried?"

"I guess he somehow imagined that he had at last found a girl who didn't care about how big his penis was … and then I went and shattered that dream."

Carlos nodded. "What do you think he'll do about it?"

"I don't know! He said he needs time to think and I'm giving it to him, but how long does he need?"

"As long as it takes. I don't think you can rush it. Just wait him out. And be nice to him."

"Oh, I am! I'm like the best wife ever! But I worry what's going on in that brain of his."

Carlos sat back and grinned at her. "And how about you? Do you feel antsy or anything?"

She caught his meaning at once. "No! I can't think about my needs at a time like this!" Her pussy was telling her something quite differently, of course.

He put the drink down and stood. He loomed over her. "As I recall, you like to feel submissive now and again."

He was testing her and she knew it. Part of her wanted to let him take her – pick her up, toss her over his shoulder and carry her down the hall to his bedroom. But the good wife wouldn't allow that – not yet, at least. Not under these circumstances.

"No," she said firmly. "Let's let this thing with my husband resolve itself before I can think about my needs again. Or yours."

He grinned and stepped back to his chair and sat. He took a sip of his drink. "Just checking."

"So you think I should just wait, no matter how long it takes?"

"Yes. To you, a week or so is plenty. To Dave, he might need a month."

"But… I can't stand not knowing!" She also wondered if she was supposed to wait a month before making love again. And yes, she meant Carlos.

"That's the difference between a woman's curiosity and a man's decision-making process. They aren't necessarily compatible."

"Yeah, thanks, Mr. Know-It-All." She shook her head. He did make her feel better. She finished her drink and stood. "Well, I'd better go. Dave should be home soon."

He stood and opened up his arms. "I at least need a hug."

She allowed herself to be enveloped and that familiar feeling of being protected washed over her. And submissive. She fought the latter and pried herself from his arms. "I have to go. I'll call you when I hear something."

She needed some space to work it all out in her head. She returned to her apartment and fixed herself another drink while she waited for Dave. When he arrived home forty minutes later, she was feeling a mellow buzz from the alcohol.

* * *

"Dave!" she said and gave him a big hug.

He eyed her warily. "What's up with you?"

"Nothing! Can't a wife welcome her husband home without suspicion?"

He picked up her empty glass. "How many of these have you had?"

"I dunno. Two or three, I guess. You want one? I can fix us both one."

"No, not right now – and I think you've had enough."

"Awww," she pouted. She sat down heavily on the couch.

"I thought we should talk, but I guess we'll wait until later."

"No, no. I'm good. Talk." She waved a hand at him.

He gave her a long look. "Well, maybe this will act like truth serum, huh?"

She grinned at him.

"Okay. I've been thinking about what happened and I've decided…" He paused to take in a slow breath, "it's okay with me as long as we follow the rules we set down."

Barb immediately shook her head. "No. I mean, yes, except for the condom part. I hate the damn things." She picked up her drink and drained the last few drops. "Oh, and maybe I'll fuck him other times, when you aren't home. Okay?"

"No, not okay!" he said, feeling the heat rise in his face. "We had a deal!"

"I know we did. And it was a good deal. And I love you. But this is how it's gonna be. I'm not going to lie to you and tell you he'll always wear a condom or we'll never see each other when you're not around. I can just see how this will develop, that's all." She slurred her S's. "Plus," she added. "I think we should get you one of those little cages."

Dave was shocked. This wasn't how it was supposed to go. He had gone back and forth at work, thinking about his desires versus Barb's and knew he would be in his right to put a stop to it, but then what? She'd just go out and find someone else someday. And maybe this next guy she'd leave him for. Due to the vast differences between Barb and Carlos, he doubted she'd ever want to run off with him, although he wasn't entirely sure. Somehow, she couldn't see Barb bringing Carlos home to her mamma and daddy and telling them they were going to get married. No, he was the safe choice, but in being so, he'd have to agree to allow her a sexual outlet now and then. Something he could control by granting or withdrawing his permission.

He had thought Barb might want to see Carlos once a week or two, just enough to scratch her itch, while remaining the dutiful wife. Now, to hear her talk, she wanted to change the deal entirely!

"This sounds like you're going back on our deal," he told her. "Maybe we should talk about it when you're sober."

"I'm not that drunk!" she insisted. "I'm just being honest. Maybe if I wasn't so drunk I'd lie to you. Is that what you want?" When he didn't speak, she added, "Like tell you we've never fucked without a condom or something."

Dave rocked back on his heels. "I think I will have that drink," he said and poured himself a stiff shot of bourbon. The bottle was nearly empty. Barb held up her glass and he shook his head. "Any more and you'll be incoherent. Tell me about the time you fucked him without a condom. I guess I wasn't there, huh?"

Barb squinted, as if trying to remember what she was supposed to admit and what was supposed to be a secret. She shrugged. "In the laundry room. And in his apartment. Just twice." She grinned at him. "It's sooo much better without a condom. He's clean, so don't worry."

"You've fucked him twice already! Jeez! You only had him over last…" He stopped when the light dawned. "Wait. How long have you guys been together?"

"Only a coupla weeks." She shook her head. "Only a coupla times."

"So you lied to me? You made me go down there and ask him to 'take care of you' when you guys had already fucked?! Jesus!"

She shrugged. "I'm sorry. I woulda tole you eventually. I don't want secrets between us. I love you. And this set-up is gonna be perfect. I have the husband I want and the big dick I need. See?" She grinned at him.

Dave took a big gulp and let the bourbon burn his throat as he contemplated his options. There weren't many. One, he could divorce Barb and try to forget about her. Let her reap what she has sown. He doubted Carlos would want to marry her, just to fuck her now and then. Didn't he say he had other women? He'd probably reject her advances and she'd either be one of his harem or have to find another sucker like him.

Although the idea appealed to him on a visceral level, he knew he didn't want to lose her. Despite everything, Dave felt he had finally found a woman who accepted him for who he was – well, almost anyway – and he loathed the idea that he'd have to go back out into the dating pool and find another woman like Barb. The humiliation when they discovered he had a small penis would be impossible to bear again.

Two, he could try and work with what he had here. Try to limit Barb's infatuation with Carlos and try to impose some sort of agreement he could live with. If that meant relaxing some rules, well, it was better than the alternative.

Her mention of a cock cage scared him, however. How did she know about that? Had he let something slip? Sure, he enjoyed looking at pictures and videos of married women with husbands locked up. But to bring those fantasies to light and live them? No. He wasn't that kind of guy. Right? He wondered if he was trying to convince himself. And why was his cock suddenly hard?

He picked up the bottle and carried it to the bar and checked to make sure they had no other liquor in the house. He went to the kitchen, took one last good slug from the mouth, and poured the rest down the sink. He put the bottle in the recycling bin. Even angry, he was a good steward of the environment.

He returned to the living room. "What did you do?" Barb asked.

"I poured the liquor. We'll talk when you're sober."

"I'm sober enough!"

"Clearly you're not. You've said some things that have hurt me and you don't even know it."

She frowned. "What? What did I say? You mean about Carlos and me? Well, you would've found out eventually. You don't want me to live a lie, do you?"

"We'll talk later. Sober up. Make some coffee. Eat something. I'll be back later." He picked up his keys and left, leaving Barb sitting there, a puzzled expression on her face.

Dave didn't know where to go, so he went to Carlos's place. It seemed odd, but he had to find out just how much the man was into his wife. Did he want to run off with her? He doubted it, but he had needed some reassurance.

He knocked on the door and Carlos looked surprised when he answered. "Oh, Dave! What can I do for you?"

"Can we talk? Are you alone?"

The big man nodded. "Sure, come in." Dave followed him in and shut the door behind himself. "Drink?"

"Yeah, I think I could use one."

"Bourbon?"

"That's fine."

He took the proffered glass and they sat across from each other. Carlos was relaxed, but wary. He waited for Dave to speak.

"Uh…" Dave started. "Barb told me the affair started earlier than what I thought. She's a little drunk and she said she didn't want to have secrets between us. I guess that's good. Maybe."

Carlos nodded. "So, you're here to demand we stop? Or to shout at me?"

"No, no. I mean, that would be great and all, but then what? I know my wife needs a guy like you. It's embarrassing, but there it is. I can't change it."

Carlos nodded again and said nothing. He sipped his drink.

"So I'm thinking about what I can do here and it's not much. I don't want to divorce my wife. I love her and she's good for me. I guess, finding out that you two have been an item for a couple of weeks or a month was a bit of a shock. She made me feel like a fool. All those rules I tried to make – they all seem silly now. So what I need to know is, do you think Barb is the kind of girl you'd want to run off with?"

The big man shook his head. "Don't get me wrong. Your wife is great. A real spitfire. But I have others, you know. I can't be exclusive."

Dave felt a wave of relief wash over him. "Great! I mean, that's what I thought. That's my biggest fear, you know, is having her leave me for someone else. You see, I'm … I'm not good at dating." He paused, trying to walk the fine line between admitting his shortcomings – ha, ha – and not revealing so much it would make him sound pathetic. He wasn't sure he had succeeded. He took a healthy sip of his drink. "Anyway, if this is just an outlet for her, I guess I can live with it. As long as we don't go too far with things."

"How do you mean?"

"I don't see myself as one of those cuckolds you see online. I mean, sure it's kinda exciting to read about, but I don't see myself like that – you know, wearing women's clothes and such. I want my wife to be happy, but I also want to retain my dignity. I'm here to ask for your help." It surprised him – he was saying pretty much the opposite of what the secret side of him wanted. He knew it was his ego talking.

"And in exchange…?"

"I'll grant you guys some latitude. Just as long as you don't run away together. Deal?"

Carlos took a sip of his bourbon and thought about it. "What do you mean by 'latitude'?"

"Uh, well, I already know you guys have fucked without condoms, so I guess that ship has sailed. You have any diseases I should know about?"

Carlos shook his head.

"All right. And I guess I don't have to be there every time. Okay?"

"Deal," he said at once, raising the glass toward Dave. "It might be good for your wife to hear about all this from you. Maybe it will keep her from falling for me in the way you describe. I like things the way they are."

"Oh, I will. I will. She's just kinda drunk tonight. I think she was feeling guilty or something. You know, about the lying and all."

"I can get that. So, we're cool then?"

Dave finished his drink. "We're cool." He stood up and reached out with his right hand. Carlos stood and shook it. "It's kinda weird, isn't it? We're making a deal so that you can continue to fuck my wife."

Carlos chuckled. "I guess so. But you'd be surprised how common this is among my buddies. Lots of white women are in the same boat. Some want to check us off their bucket list one time, but others want a steady supply of BBC, if you know what I mean."

"Maybe she'll get this out of her system."

"Maybe," Carlos said, but his tone indicated he doubted it.

Chapter Nine

Barb wondered where Dave had gone – it had been over an hour since he had left. Maybe to a bar – or back to work. He always had papers to grade. She felt guilty – she shouldn't have said those things. It was too soon. But she had allowed the liquor to talk for her. She got up and walked a bit unsteadily to the kitchen. Damn! It wasn't like her to drink so much. She didn't want to become a lush. She poured herself a glass of water and drank it, trying to dilute the liquor in her system.

I really should eat something, she thought and found a bowl half-filled with a day-old casserole. She grabbed a fork and ate a couple of bites cold and put the rest back. Not in the mood for that.

She returned to the couch and lay down, trying to keep the room from spinning. In minutes, she was asleep. She woke up later, seeing how the shadows had changed on the wall. The sun had nearly set. She heard the door close and realized Dave had returned. She sat up, her head clearer now.

"Dave?"

"Yeah," he said, coming in. "You okay?"

"Yeah. I was worried. Where did you go?"

"Just back to the office for awhile. I thought we needed some space so you could, uh, recover."

"God. I'm sorry about that. I don't usually drink so much."

"I know. But I know why you did."

"What did I say? I felt like I said something I shouldn't't've."

"You don't remember?" Dave sat across from her.

"Uhh, I'm afraid to remember."

"You pretty much told me everything. About how you've been fucking Carlos for weeks and you haven't used condoms…"

"Oh god…" She put her head in her hands.

"Don't worry about it. I think your conscience was bothering you. I'm glad it's all out in the open."

"Really?"

"Yeah." He leaned forward and put his elbows on his knees. "I talked to Carlos."

Barb's mouth dropped open. "What did you do? You guys didn't …"

"What, fight?" He gave a barking laugh. "Hardly. He was a perfect gentleman. And I was too, of course."

"What did you talk about?"

"The rules, I guess. Or the parameters. Whatever."

She sat back. "So what have you two decided about my sex life?"

"Oh, relax. You were drunk. You said some things that upset me, so I went to the source while you sobered up."

"I'm sorry if I hurt you."

He waved it away. "I know you are. You say you love me, I think you felt you had to tell me the truth. I guess I'm good with that."

"But…"

"The upshot of all this is that you can fuck Carlos anytime you want. Whether I'm there or not. And I know you haven't used condoms before, so that's out too. Just remain on the pill, of course."

"Of course."

"My only worry is that you don't run off with him and leave me."

"Oh, I would never do that!"

"Yeah, that's what Carlos said. He said he likes things the way they are. He doesn't want to be exclusive."

That revelation gave her a twinge – not that she could ever run off with Carlos! But she did like the idea that he'd be waiting for her whenever she needed him. Now she realized she'd have to fit into his busy schedule of floozies like Darlene and other married whores like her.

"Okay," was all she said.

"And lastly, this isn't going to be like those fantasies you read about online. I'm not going to be your servant or wear one of those ridiculous cages."

Barb colored. "I said that?"

"You did. And I think you weren't kidding. But that's not me, okay? So... deal?"

She nodded, then paused. "Wait. Just so we're clear: You're okay if I go down to see Carlos any time or have him over here, just as long as we treat you with respect?"

"Pretty much. I mean, I'd like to be there, of course. So we can work that out. But bottom line, I won't be your sycophantic cuckold who wears women's underwear and has his cock all caged up."

"Ewww! I would never ask you to do that!" But inside, she was feeling a bit disappointed. Those fantasies had aroused her and she couldn't deny it. Still, half a loaf was better than none. "Okay, it's a deal."

"Good. Now, what's for dinner?"

* * *

Barb took advantage of their deal two days later, on a Sunday. She had called Carlos first, of course. She didn't want to barge in on him. But the itch had returned and she needed a good scratching. He had been free and told her to come down around noon. Dave had gone out to play golf, so he would be out of the way. She didn't tell him what she would be doing – she didn't want to hurt him. Besides, it wouldn't help him concentrate on his golf game.

She spent an hour in the bathroom, trimming her pubes to a neat triangle and showering. She dabbed on some perfume and felt pretty damn sexy before she headed downstairs.

She knocked on the door and Carlos grinned wolfishly at her. He grabbed her arm and pulled her inside and she immediately let go of her "good wife" persona and allowed the slutty, submissive side to surface. He enveloped her in his muscular arms and kissed her. He bent down and picked her up easily and kicked the door closed with his foot. He carried her down the hall to his bedroom and tossed her on the bed. He attacked her, removing her clothes as if he couldn't wait to have her.

"Wait, wait!" she cried, "Don't rip them!"

"You wear too many clothes," he told her. "I'd rather see you come down in next to nothing."

"I can't!" She protested as she found herself quickly naked. "What if someone saw me!?"

"That would be part of the thrill, the risk of being caught."

She nodded, thinking maybe a nice robe with nothing on underneath or zip-up dress with no underwear. It sounded so hot and nasty! Her thoughts were interrupted when he started stripping off his clothes. This was a sight not to be missed. When he cock came into view, it was already half-hard.

"Suck it," he demanded and she fell on it as if her life depended on it. He tasted musky and sexy and her pussy began dripping almost at once. She made love to his cock, rubbing the shaft with her hand while her mouth took in as much of the head as she could. His cock swelled. God he was big! She had to have him!

"Damn, you make me so horny!" she cried and threw

herself back onto the bed, spreading her legs. She wondered if he'd notice she'd trimmed up.

He was on her in a flash, kissing her, biting her nipples, his hands pawing her hot flesh. Barb pulled her legs wide apart as if to say, *I'm ready! Fuck me!* and she soon felt the bulbous tip of his cock spread apart her wet lips. It gushed with new fluids and she could feel her hips crack before he was fully into her.

"Yes!" she cried as more of his shaft slid in. "Oh, god yes!"

Carlos proceeded to fuck the shit out of her and she hung on, orgasm after orgasm rolling through her. Her mouth came open, she drooled and made gibberish noises.

"Uh, uh, uh, fuck, shit, god damn! Oh, oh! Uh, uh, uh…" and on until she could feel Carlos stiffen over her and suddenly, he thrust deep and she could feel his cock releasing its seed into her womb.

"FUCK!" she screamed and clung to him until the last of her orgasms faded away.

Carlos grunted and rolled to the side. His body was sweaty and she wanted to rub it all over her body, get closer to him, if that was possible. She snuggled up to him and said, "Wow."

He grinned and hooked an arm around her shoulder and pulled her close. "You liked that, huh?"

"Oh my god, I've never felt anything like it. I mean, I love my husband, but fuck!"

"Lot of women live lives of quiet desperation," he said.

For some reason, that stirred up pangs of jealousy in her. "Tell me about your other women."

He tipped his head back and gave her a look. "I don't think so."

"Why not? I'm not jealous or anything," she lied.

He laughed. "Sure you aren't."

"Well, maybe a little," she admitted. "But after such a

powerful session, a gal just likes to know where she stands, that's all."

"You stand with your husband. I'm just the occasional handy man."

"I know that! I'm not asking for you to be exclusive to me. I'm just curious. I'd like to know how they are ... different from me and all."

"Would you want me to tell them intimate details about you?"

"Uh, no, I guess not."

"There ya go."

Barb was persistent. "Okay. Just give me a general sense, then. First of all, how many others are there? I mean besides the married one you already told me about."

He gave her another sideways glance. "Just two. One married and one not."

"Ohh, Darlene, the floozy – she's the one not married, right?"

"She's not a floozy."

"Oh, sorry. I guess I didn't mean to say that out loud."

"She's very nice."

"Do you see you guys, uh, becoming exclusive?"

He chuckled. "You worried I'll drop you?"

"No... well, maybe yes. I mean, I feel lucky to have found you."

"And if I fall by the wayside, there will be another man to take my place. Now that you've tasted the sweet nectar of black love, you'll find you can't go back to regular white-boy sex."

"You make it sound like you're so easily replaceable."

"No, of course I'm not," he said. "But I've found these things tend to have an expiration date."

"Really? Do they end badly?"

"Sometimes, yes. Sometimes the husband gets jealous or they find someone new who is a better fit..."

"I can't imagine anyone who fits me better than you," she interjected.

"Or if they're single, you find things that you don't quite agree on and you drift apart. It's not all about sex, you know."

"I know. I know this is temporary, although I would hate to see it end! I mean, we just got started."

"I think that depends on you and your husband."

"You think he'll get jealous?"

"I think he's already jealous. He puts on a brave face, trying to give you what you want. But over time, it will probably eat at him."

"And then what? I mean, from your experience."

"The wife has to choose and it's really not choice. I'm not going to run off with the woman – not my style – so she goes back to her husband and lives a sadder life, I guess." He paused. "Or, she finds another guy to sneak around with."

"You think I could ever come back and sneak around with you?"

"I find that to be dangerous. In the case of a married woman who wants to explore her sexuality, I find it's best to bring it out in the open. If the husband objects, I'm gone. Too many jealous men have guns nowadays."

She nodded. She couldn't imagine Dave ever being jealous enough to shoot someone, but she had read about it. "It seems Dave is on board with us."

"For now," Carlos said.

Barb pushed herself up on one elbow. "You think it won't last?"

He shrugged. "Hard to tell. He clearly loves you and wants you to have a good sex life and he knows he can't give you that. So it's great that he's man enough to let you find another lover. But the guy has to get his own needs met too, you know."

Barb nodded. "I can see that. What should I do in Dave' case – let him fuck me whenever he wants?"

"Sure. For now, anyway. But I'm not sure that would satisfy him because he'll know you aren't really feeling it." He paused. "Or you could go the other way…"

"What do you mean?"

"I know he said he doesn't want to be cuckolded and humiliated, but sometimes, that's just his ego talking. Deep down, he might like to be treated that way. It might be a way for him to get sexually satisfied."

"But you heard him! He said he wasn't into all that stuff!"

Carlos shrugged. "I know. And he might mean it. I'm just sayin', I don't see what Dave is getting out of all of this."

Barb nodded, thinking he was probably right. Dave had been magnanimous about letting her fuck Carlos whenever she wanted, as long as she didn't leave him. Well, there was little danger in that! Carlos had made it clear he wasn't going to be exclusive. So what was Dave getting out of this? Freedom to play more golf?

"He did seem to like all those websites," she said, thinking out loud.

"That may be your clue. See what he's looking at now, after you're coming down to fuck me regularly. If he's still looking at those sites that show cuckolds being humiliated and such, maybe he's saying one thing and thinking another."

"Huh. I never thought of it that way."

"Well, it's early yet. Hell, he may get jealous and tell you he can't stand the idea of you seeing me any more, so you got to be prepared. You may have to become more, uh, forceful with him. In the meantime, you should figure out what he needs to be happy in this situation. If the man is just doing this to please his wife and isn't getting anything out of it but anxiety, trouble will follow, I guarantee it."

"Wow. You've given me a lot to think about. I'm not sure what I should do."

"Start by letting him fuck you whenever he wants. That

might satisfy his ego some. But also, push him a little in the other direction."

"How do you mean?"

"Make him clean up after himself all the time – get him used to the taste of sperm. See if he objects. If he doesn't, make him clean you up after we make love. You'll have to be sly – maybe don't tell him the first time. But just see how he reacts."

Barb nodded. "I get it. See if his words match his deeds."

"Right. If he lets you push him down that road, keep going. Remember, you heard his ego talking, not his id. And the id is the more powerful force in a man's sexuality."

Barb slid down and kissed his semen-soaked cock. "And what about your sexuality? Think you could go again?"

Carlos laughed. "Maybe if you keep doin' that, yeah."

Barb smiled and got to work.

Chapter Ten

Barb didn't shower when she returned to her apartment. She wanted to test her husband, to see how he reacted to smelling Carlos on her. She didn't expect he'd want to clean her up, but observing his response would go a long way to seeing how deep his fetish ran.

Dave had played just nine holes at Forest Park, as was his custom, and returned forty-five minutes later.

"Hi, hon!" she said cheerfully and gave him a hug.

If he noticed anything different about her, he didn't say. "Hi," he said.

"Have a good game?"

"Yes, I did. Shot a forty!" For him, that was good. "How about you? What did you do?"

"I went down and visited Carlos," she said.

His eyebrows rose up. "Oh, really?"

"Yeah." She grinned. "You want sloppy seconds?"

Something in his eyes changed. "Uh, yeah. I do."

She took his arm and led him down the hall. "But I just got off the golf course! I need to shower first!" he protested.

"Don't bother. I didn't."

His mouth dropped open but she didn't hear any protests. They quickly stripped, yanked back the covers and climbed into bed.

"You... really didn't shower?" he asked.

"No. Can you smell him?"

He bent down and sniffed. "Yeah, I can, actually."

"I'm really messy down there, too," she added, spreading apart her legs.

"I can see that." He didn't offer to clean her up and she didn't press it. He kissed her. "Tell me about it."

"Oh? You want to hear the gory details? How his big dick spread me apart and how many times I came?"

"Yeah," he said breathlessly. "I mean, that's part of it, you know. If I'm going to live vicariously through Carlos, I need to hear about it. Besides, I don't want you sneaking around. I'm glad you told me. I just wish I could've been there."

"You will be, sometimes. But other times, our schedules might not line up."

He nodded. "So, tell me."

"Ohh," she began and described how Carlos's cock tasted and how it felt going in. She told him she lost count of her orgasms. She noted while she was talking, Dave was running his hands all over her body. His little dick was hard and she felt a sudden urge to suck on it, something she only did on special occasions. When she bent down and took it into her mouth, it began to wither. He pushed her away.

"You don't have to do that."

She looked up. "Why not? I thought you liked it?"

"Well, yeah, I do, but..."

"What?"

"I can't help but feel you comparing my dick to his and it kinda kills the mood."

"Ohh." Barb understood now. She lay back. "So you wanna fuck me now?"

He grinned. "Yeah. But keep talking. It's kinda sexy."

She nodded and added some new details she had forgotten before. It surprised her that he was so turned on by all of this. She had half-expected him to get angry or feel inadequate to the point he couldn't perform. Yet the more she talked about fucking Carlos, the harder he got.

When he slipped himself inside her, she could barely feel it. But she pretended she did and acted like he was as big as Carlos, even though she was sure he would know she was exaggerating. Somehow, he didn't seem to care. He listened to her talk as he rutted with her and used his fingers to help himself. Within two minutes, he climaxed, squirting his seed into her. He rolled off and gasped for air.

"That was really good, honey!" she cooed.

He waved a hand. "You don't have to say that – I know you didn't come."

"Maybe I'm just worn out. But you seemed to really enjoy it."

"Yeah, it was nice."

Barb had a sudden thought and knew it was a bit risky. But why not? She asked, "Maybe you could help me to come, huh?"

He turned to look at her. "You mean…?"

"Yeah. You've done it before."

"Sure, but not… you know… after."

"Usually, you're sound asleep after. But you seem to have some energy now."

"I mean after… you know… Carlos. I assume you guys didn't use a condom."

"No, we didn't."

"See? That's what I mean. I'm not… you know…"

"Well, I find it very sexy for you to do that. Maybe some day, you might clean me up after you come? It would really turn me on."

"Really? Hmm. I didn't know that."

"That's because we usually make love at night and you're pretty tired. Maybe if we made love during the day, you might stay awake long enough to help me out."

"Hmm."

She didn't press it. She wanted to let the wheels go around in her husband's head.

* * *

Dave couldn't believe it. His wife had asked him to clean her up – after she'd been with Carlos! It had taken all his willpower not to dive in. He was afraid she might think him some sort of freak. What kind of husband does that, anyway? He was an accomplished educator! He couldn't be doing something so wicked and nasty! Could he?

God, he had wanted to – and it scared him a little. He loved fucking her after Carlos had been inside her, leaving his seed for his dick to wallow in. And wallow was the right word – he could already tell she was stretched out. He had to use his fingers to create enough friction to come. He couldn't quite figure out why that didn't bother him. Maybe he was beginning to embrace the cuckold lifestyle.

* * *

During the following week, Dave didn't make any advances toward Barb and she didn't press him. She wasn't able to connect with Carlos, either. She had called him Thursday, but he begged off, telling her he'd see her this weekend. By Saturday, she was feeling antsy again. Something about having great sex did that to her. While sitting around having coffee, she mentioned it to Dave.

"I'm feeling neglected, honey."

"Oh? Carlos busy?"

"Yeah. But I'm also feeling sexy around you more lately. It's like I'm in love all over again."

"Aww, that's nice. I'm glad."

"I think it's because you gave your permission for me to fool around. I feel like I'm the luckiest gal in the world."

"Good." He didn't exactly seem in the mood.

She tried again. "Sooo, I was wondering…" She batted her eyes at him.

"Oh? You want me? I figured you'd want to make an arrangement with Carlos."

"No, silly!"

He snapped his fingers. "He must be busy! So you have to settle for me."

She punched his arm. "No! It's not like that! I'm just feeling really randy and happy and grateful and I want to share all that with my husband. Okay?"

"Right now? I was going to clean the gutters or something." He was kidding, of course. Barb knew he was just trying to get a rise out of her. She refused to take the bait.

"I guess if you're not interested..."

"I didn't say that!" he put in quickly. "But please tell me what's going on with Carlos."

"I don't know – I haven't seen him lately. He's been busy. We're supposed to connect this weekend. Maybe you could be there, hm?"

He gave her a lewd grin. "Yeah, that would be nice."

"In the meantime, I'd very much like to spend some quality time with my husband."

He shrugged, finished his coffee and stood up. "Okay." He held out his hand. She took it, a smile spreading over her face. He seemed distant somehow and she was trying to ignore it by being positive.

He led her down the hallway and into the bedroom. Their clothes came off again. Already his penis was erect and she felt an urge to suck on it. She wondered if she should. Would he feel inadequate again? She decided to let him take the lead.

He pulled the covers back and they slid in. He held her and kissed her and she could feel his cock press against her thigh. Although she had never measured it, she guessed it was about four inches long, fully erect. Three inches shorter than Carlos and much thinner. It was the thinness that made all the difference. A woman just needs some girth, damn it!

He kissed her and nibbled on her breasts for a few minutes, giving her his standard tour of her body until he could position himself over her. She didn't demand he take care of her first – she wanted to test out Carlos's theory. Dave slipped himself inside her and, once again, she hardly felt him. She must've really been stretched out already by her new lover. She made all the right noises, but Dave was having some trouble with friction and had to reach down to use his fingers to stimulate his member. They rutted like an old Model T, bucking and jerking until he suddenly stopped and rolled away.

"What?" she said at once, alarmed. She knew he hadn't come.

"I don't think you can feel me anymore," he said, sadness in his voice like he was talking about a lost dog.

"I'm sorry! Maybe I could–" She reached for him.

"No," he said, turning away. "It's all right."

"No it's not! I don't want you to lose anything here. This is supposed to be good for both of us!"

"I'm not exactly sure how it's good for me. I can't satisfy you, so you get a bigger guy and now your pussy belongs to him, that's all."

"No, it's not all! There are other ways to make love! Or I could do Kegel exercises, you know, tighten up…"

"It's all right. I know my place."

Barb wasn't sure what to do. Then she remembered what she had read about cuckolds and how they actually got off on this anxiety that was created when their wives were enjoying other men. It would mean she'd have to be more dominant, something she wasn't sure she could pull off. But she had to try.

"Come," she said, waving him closer. She spread her legs. "Kneel here."

"What?" But he did as she asked.

"Now, take your dick in hand and squirt all over me."

"What?"

"Come on! You heard me! I want you to come on me!"

Her tone had the desired effect. He knelt close and his

hand began to rub his cock.

"Ohhh, yeah, that's it, baby, I love to see you jack off. I want you to squirt it all over me!"

He grew excited and his little cock seemed to grow in his hand.

"Tell me about you and Carlos," he gasped.

She suddenly got it. He got turned on by hearing about her trysts. "Oh, his cock really stretches me! I see stars whenever he fucks me. It's as if I can feel every vein and bump!"

He tipped it down and gasped and Barb felt his watery discharge squirt over the entrance to her pussy. He gasped and rolled to the side. She gave him a few minutes and said: "I want to come now." It wasn't stated as a request.

There was silence for a minute before he spoke. "You mean…?"

"Of course. I mean, you got to come. Usually I make you go first. I'm just really horny from watching you."

"That turned you on?" He seemed surprised.

"Of course. Now get busy!" She tried to sound commanding.

Dave hesitated. "It's just… I came."

She pretended to get angry. "So? It's not a big deal! I've given you plenty of blow-jobs!"

"Okay, okay! Don't get all mad." He rolled over and crawled between her legs. He seemed to be eyeing the mess there.

"My god, Dave! You act like it's poison or something!"

"No, no. It's fine." He bent down and gave her vagina a tentative lick. He cocked his head and tasted her again. "Hmm."

"See, I'll bet you can't even taste it!"

"No, I can't." He resumed licking her. Barb spread her legs and began to coach him, telling him to use his tongue to clean up his own mess while using fingers to excite her. Watching him lick up the white discharge excited her in ways she hadn't expected. She could feel the first tendrils of an orgasm approaching and it delighted her. Not just because she could still enjoy making love to her husband, but also the illicit nature of the act – making him bring her off while licking up his own seed. Barb's imagination ran with the idea, thinking about what it would be like to have Dave clean her up after Carlos came in her. The orgasm rushed forward and she loved the naughtiness of it all. She pictured Carlos's big cock squirting deep inside her while Dave watched. As soon as Carlos pulled out, Dave would be right there, licking and sucking, slurping up the man's seed...

"Oh god! Oh my god! Oh fuck, honey!"

The orgasm crashed over her and she jerked her thighs together against Dave's head. He pulled free and looked down at her. When she was able to focus, she could see he seemed pleased with himself.

"Oh, honey! That was great!"

"Glad to know I still have it," he said, grinning, his face smeared with their juices. "Maybe you won't need Carlos after all."

"Maybe not," she lied. "But let's not jump to conclusions yet. It's new and all."

"Sure," he said, his doubt returning to his face.

"Please, honey, I hope you can understand."

"I do. I do. It was just nice, you know. It was like the old days, in a way."

In the old days, I faked it, she thought. "I think it's the combination of my two lovers that makes my orgasms more powerful. I think it's a good thing, don't you?"

"Sure. I mean, I want you to be happy."

"Didn't you like it?"

"Yes, of course! I'm glad you're still interested in me, that's all. I would think that I'd fall by the wayside."

She hugged him. "I'll always be interested in you, dear. I love you."

"And I love you too." His words were mechanical.

Barb could tell her husband was feeling the strain from their new situation, but she wasn't sure how to fix it. Would she have to give up Carlos? She could almost hear her pussy cry out, "NO!"

Two hours later, Dave ran out to meet a colleague for lunch to discuss ways for the man to get tenure. Barb briefly wondered if he was really meeting a woman colleague and not for business and decided she was hardly in a position to be jealous.

As soon as he left, she called Carlos. He answered his cell phone and told her he was out and wouldn't be back until late afternoon. He said he was free that night and maybe she could come down and see him?

"Uhh," she said, thinking fast. "I think Dave would like to be involved this time. He's been feeling a bit left out."

There came a pause and she wondered if he would beg off. But at last he said, "Sure." They decided on seven. Barb's pussy began to throb, despite her earlier orgasm.

* * *

They all sat around the apartment, looking like gunslingers, each waiting for the other to make the first move. Barb realized it would have to be her. Dave was watching Carlos like a rabbit might stare at a coyote. Carlos was paying most of his attention to Barb, but he'd glance now and then at Dave with a dismissive smirk.

Their big happy family was coming apart and it had only been a couple of weeks!

"Hey," she said and they both looked at her. "Let's clear the air here. I see things going sideways already. Let's talk this through. Dave, I sense that you're feeling, uh, left out or something."

He flared briefly and sagged back down. "Well, how would you feel if I had to go find another girl because you didn't do it for me?" He didn't look at Carlos.

"If it was because there was something …" she almost said 'wrong with me' but caught herself in time, "…about my body that you didn't entirely like, I guess I would be feeling just like you. But because I love you, I'd work it out."

He harrumphed and didn't respond.

"Look," she tried again, "Carlos is just helping me out, that's all!" She smiled at him and he smiled back. "Don't you want me to be happy?"

"Sure, but not at my expense."

"Do you want to call this off?" Again her pussy spasmed at the very notion.

"No, I guess not. I mean, you'd either resent me or go out and find another guy."

"You might be right. And I think Carlos is the perfect guy for all this. He's already told me he doesn't want to be exclusive – he has other women!" She tried to ignore the jealousy that surfaced again. "He's just being a good guy. Can't you see that?"

"I guess." Dave glanced at Carlos and Carlos had the decency not to smirk. "I just wish…" He stopped and shrugged.

"I know, honey, I know. But this situation is not unlike the one I faced a few years ago. Remember when you got the job at Brooklyn U and we had to move from Manhattan? I had my friends there, my job? But I packed up and moved to be with you. I've learned to make new friends, find a new job."

He nodded. "I know. I'm sorry. I didn't think of it that way."

"You should! You're just letting jealousy get in the way."

"Maybe you're right. It's kinda hard not to."

"I understand. But Carlos is just like a vibrator – something I need in order to feel fulfilled." She gave Carlos a wink that Dave couldn't see. Carlos gave her a tiny nod back.

"He's kind of a big vibrator," Dave said.

"I know. But you liked it, the first time you watched – I could tell."

Dave blushed. "Yeah, maybe."

"So we're going to do it again. If you want to watch, fine. If you'd rather pout, you can stay out here." She stood and nodded at Carlos, who got to his feet as well.

"No, no – I'll come. You guys go ahead and I'll be along."

Barb held out her hand and Carlos took it. They went down the short hallway to the bedroom. She was glad they had a few minutes to themselves.

"You okay with all of this?" she asked him as they stripped out of their clothes.

He shrugged. "I'm just here to fuck the misses," he said. "If you guys can't work it out, I'll just mosey along."

She nodded. She lowered her voice to a whisper. "I've been doing what you said, you know, pushing him a bit and I think you were right – that it was just his ego talking. I think he'd kind of like to be more of the cuckold. We just have to get him past the image of what he thought he was."

Carlos nodded. "Great. Now, enough talk." He picked her up and put her on the bed and Barb felt that immediate sense of power he exuded. It made her wetter, if that was possible. Her legs fell apart and she welcomed him into her arms.

They hardly noticed when Dave slipped in and sat in a chair at the end of the bed. Carlos spent longer on foreplay, driving Barb crazy with lust as he kissed her neck, her breasts and her nipples while she writhed under him, making a puddle between her legs.

When Carlos finally got into position over her, she spread her legs wide and looked past him to see Dave and she wondered how this scene was affecting him. Would he be able to handle it? She tried not to let his angst affect her pleasure and turned her attention back to Carlos. She felt his beautiful cock spread her lips and moaned as his thick shaft force its way inside her.

"Oh god," she gasped. "Oh my god."

He eased himself deeper into her and her mouth came open as if to help. She hooked her heels around his thighs and said, "God, fuck me, you big black bastard!"

Carlos obliged, pulling back and thrusting in hard, bottoming himself out and slapping his heavy balls against her ass. She felt an orgasm swell and hung on for the ride. Dave no longer mattered – it was just Carlos and his wonderful cock, spreading her pussy apart and sending waves of heat up into her stomach and breasts.

"Fuck me," she gasped. "You're so big!"

Carlos sped up and the orgasms began, one after another. Barb lost cohesive thought and babbled while he fucked her. When she felt him stiffen, she hugged him close and his cock throbbed deep within her, sending gouts of his seed into her womb. It was the most erotic thing she had ever experienced.

When at last Carlos rolled off of her, she looked down to see Dave, with his cock out, rubbing frantically. He spotted her and quickly tucked it back into his pants.

"Don't stop on my account," she purred and he blushed.

Carlos looked around, too late to see what was going on. He shrugged and returned his attention to Barb. "That was wonderful," he told her.

"God yes. It was amazing. Thank you."

They lay there and chatted for a few minutes. Dave was not part of their conversation. They talked about the next time they could get together, as if Dave's opinion did not matter, which, it probably didn't.

Carlos glanced up at the bedside clock. "Well, I'd better go. I'm sure you guys have some things to talk about."

It brought Barb up short. "Oh, yes." She looked at Dave, who had been sitting there patiently. "Sorry, honey."

He shrugged. Carlos got up and dressed and bent down to kiss Barb, holding one of his big hands gently against her cheek. "See ya later, babe." He left.

Barb suddenly felt self-conscious and started to get up.

"Wait," Dave said and stood. He began stripping off his clothes.

Barb, who could feel Carlos seed seeping out of her, wondered why he'd want to do this now. "Really?" she asked.

"Yes. I didn't come – I just played around. I'm really horny now."

She nodded and lay back. She could see the sheen of Carlos's semen between her legs and had a sudden devilish thought.

"Oh, but I'm such a mess," she told him as he crawled up on the bed. "Maybe you could clean me up, huh?"

He frowned and gave a tiny shake of his head. She didn't push it and allowed him to lay over her and thrust his small penis inside. She barely felt it. Like before, Dave had to use his own fingers to create friction. He was clearly excited because within a couple of minutes, he grunted and she felt his discharge leak from her gaping pussy and stain the sheets.

She tried again. "Oh, honey – I didn't come. But I usually do on your tongue. You're so good at it."

He pushed himself back and stared at the mess for a moment. She watched him lick his lips.

"I really love the orgasms you give me," she encouraged him.

He nodded. "Don't tell anyone," he said at last and bent down to give her clit a tentative lick.

"I won't, I promise," she said, wondering if that was a promise she could keep. She marveled at the change in her husband. She never would have guessed that he'd ever agree to clean her up after Carlos. Any further thoughts on the subject were pushed away by the feelings radiating out from her clit.

"Oh! Oh yes!" He was getting good at this. "More!"

He seemed not to care about the mess and dug his tongue deeper into her, then came up to tease her clit. It was having the desired effect. Barb lifted her hips to help him and felt another orgasm stirring within her.

"Oh, god, honey! Yes! Do that! Oh fuck!"

The climax rocked her and she slapped her thighs tight around Dave's head. Her body shook and she saw stars for a moment. Dave waited patiently for her to relax before extricating himself from between her legs.

"Oh my god, honey! That was... Oh god!"

He grinned down at her, his face smeared with juices. "Glad you liked it."

"Oh, you don't know how good that was! Fuck!" She wasn't just being nice. Something about oral sex under those conditions really made her come hard.

"Was it as good as...?" He trailed off.

"Oh god yes! Oh my god! Come here!" She opened her arms and he came to her. She kissed his face, enjoying the sensation of the slippery mess that covered his mouth and chin. She hugged him tightly. "Fuck!"

"I'm glad," he said. "I'm glad you liked it." He seemed pretty pleased with himself.

Chapter Eleven

Later, after they had showered, dressed and were sitting on the couch with glasses of wine, they discussed what had just happened.

"I'm not sure if I can explain it," she said. "Sure, Carlos is a good lover – you know that. But, god! Having you do that to me just sent me to the moon! I'm not even sure why." She knew why, she was just being coy.

"I guess it was the naughty factor or something."

"How do you mean?" She wanted him to say it.

"You know – not many husbands would do that. I mean, he had just come in you and all…"

"I guess. You might be right. I'm very glad you did because that orgasm was every bit as powerful as the others." She wasn't entirely sure about that, but she knew it would sound good to Dave. In her mind, it had been very pleasurable, but knowing her husband was, in essence, cleaning up after her lover drove her orgasm to new heights.

"It was kinda sexy. And nasty."

"Yeah. I'm a very happy girl right now."

He nodded and sipped his wine.

She added, "Are you okay with all of this? I mean, I want you to be happy too."

"Yeah, I am. I'm just adjusting, that's all. At first, it

was tough, you know. I wish I was normal and all. But I've learned over the years that I have to accept the way things are. It's nice, in a way, to have Carlos around. I can kinda pretend it's me fucking you. I know that probably sounds pathetic, but..."

"No! Not at all! It's great! I'm glad you can enjoy watching us."

"Yeah. It was hard at first, but I'm getting used to it."

"It was the after part that really sent me. You surprised me."

"I surprised myself. I'm not sure what came over me."

Barb leaned forward and gave her husband a loving kiss. "I loved it. You can make me come anytime."

He nodded and they clinked their glasses together.

"He asked me not to tell, so I won't. I'll let him tell you. Or maybe he'll show you someday," she told Carlos the next day. They were sitting in his apartment, an hour before Dave was due home from work. She had told Carlos as soon as she showed up that she wasn't interested in sex – she just wanted to talk. Carlos was still dressed in his suit pants, dress shirt and tie and for some reason, it made her horny just to look at him. She still had just come from work herself and had on a conservative skirt, stockings and blouse. He invited her in and asked if she wanted a beer. She declined.

They sat opposite each other while Barb tried to explain what had happened yesterday after Carlos had left without betraying her husband's confidence.

"It seems Dave is starting to embrace the idea of having you around," she told him. "We made love afterward and it was pretty good." It wasn't the fucking that was good, but she didn't want to give away too many details.

"I'm glad," he said, although his puzzled expression showed he didn't understand how that was possible.

"I think it was the fact that he fucked me while I was all

messy that made it better."

He nodded. "I see. And you could feel him?"

She shrugged. "Sorta. But he took care of me and that made it good."

"Oh, I see." He smiled and seemed to understand what the secret was all about. "But he doesn't want you to talk about it?"

"I think it's just him being a little embarrassed. You know."

He gave a slow nod. "I do. Give it time. Pretty soon, he'll let all that go."

"You think?"

"Yes. Keep encouraging him. Eventually, he'll want to participate, you know. While I'm still there."

"Really?" Barb couldn't imagine Dave cleaning her up and giving her another orgasm while Carlos watched.

"It will depend on how we act too. I've seen husbands like Dave before. Their ego is fragile because they don't feel like real men. But if they can make their wives come other ways… well, then they feel better about themselves. If you mock them during this early stage, it might all come crashing down."

"I would never do that! And I'm sure you wouldn't either."

"No, but then I'm still observing the dynamic. It really depends on the guy, you see. Some guys like that kind of abuse. The cuckold angst, if you will. They like it when their wives ridicule them. They like being forced to wait on the bull like a servant. They liked being locked up in those little cages and dressed up in panties and all. I'm not sure Dave is that guy – he says he isn't – but that all remains to be seen."

"I'm not sure I see Dave in that way, either."

"You never know. Just keep pushing him. You can always back off if he gets angry or starts pouting. For now, just encourage him and see where it goes."

"Okay. Well, I'd better go. He'll be home soon." She stood.

He stood and spread out his arms. She allowed herself to be hugged and instantly her pussy grew wetter just from this simple embrace. When one of his hands slipped down to her ass and gripped it, she tried to extract herself but he wouldn't budge. She was fighting against her own conscience and feared she might lose.

"I should go."

"In a minute," he said, now both hands caressing her bottom. She shivered.

His hands pulled up the skirt and fondled her bottom through her thin panties.

"Carlos," she warned but it was parrot talk, something she felt she should say. They had just made love yesterday, they couldn't possibly do it again today! Besides, Dave would be home in a half-hour or so...

One of his hands slipped around to the front of her panties and she gasped.

"Ohh, you're all wet here," he said and she knew she was lost.

Without saying another word, Carlos unbuckled his pants and freed his cock. She tried to pull away, but his other hand kept her in place. Both hands returned to her bottom and he easily lifted her up. She felt his hard shaft against the gusset of her panties and gasped again.

"No!" she said but she didn't mean it and she didn't want him to stop. She liked being taken, as if she was so desirable, he couldn't help himself. She felt the tip of his hard cock probing her, pressing against the panties and she didn't want them ripped. As soon as she reached down to ease them aside, she knew she was giving her acquiescence to being fucked.

His cock slipped into her at once and she moaned and bit his shoulder through his shirt. Being held up like this while he fucked her was a new experience for her and she felt so helpless it made her submissiveness leap forward. She was his to do as he pleased. She could only hang on as he took his pleasure.

He lifted her up and down on his cock, driving himself deeper into her and the spots began dancing in front of her eyes.

"Fuck, fuck, fuck..." she babbled. She could hear him grunting with effort and it made her crazy with lust. Her orgasms shot through her and she could only hang on until Carlos was done with her.

His strength was amazing. She felt so light in his arms, his cock alternating with his arms to do the lifting. She could feel his cock push her up as he drove himself fully into her, then his arms held her as it withdrew, only for the process to start again. Barb thought she might lose her fucking mind.

"Fuck me, fuck me, fuck me, FUCK ME!" she cried out, her body like a toy on this big man's cock.

Suddenly, he stiffened and she gasped, feeling every throb of his cock squirting his seed deep into her womb. It triggered a final orgasm and she bit hard on his shoulder, her body shaking.

Carlos turned her around and eased her down on the upholstered chair. He slid out and she felt the fluids begin to leak. She covered her pussy with her hand and said, "I don't want to make a mess on your furniture."

He laughed and grabbed a kitchen towel from the nearby table. She used it to sop up the mess. "Fuck, you came a lot!"

"You do that to me."

"But we just fucked yesterday!"

He chuckled. "Guess I have excellent regenerative abilities."

"God, for a black guy, you use a lot of big words," she teased him.

"It's all the training I'm getting from those Wall Street white boys," he joked.

"How am I supposed to go home now, all messed up? I don't know if I have time to take a shower."

"I would suggest you don't. And spread your legs and tell him you loved what he did for you yesterday and could he do it again?"

"You think he'd go for it?"

"You might be surprised. Hey, the worst that could happen is he'll refuse and you go in and take a shower."

"Huh." She wouldn't have thought of that on her own. She would have assumed he'd be mad that she fucked Carlos again so soon and she would have snuck in for a quick shower first. "You think?"

He shrugged. "Worth a try."

"He could be shocked at my slutty behavior."

"Just tell him you only came up to talk and that I forced myself on you. That much is true."

"Yeah, but I hardly resisted."

"That's because it's still new. Don't worry – you'll grow tired of me eventually."

"I don't see that happening anytime soon. You do something to me on a visceral level that I can't seem to resist." She stood, still clutching the towel between her legs.

"Go. Try out my theory. Let me know how it goes."

"Okay, if you say so." She handed him the towel and kissed him. He held her tight and she wondered if he might want to fuck her again. She was game. But he opened the door and the moment was lost. Barb clenched her pussy tightly and took the elevator up to her place. She could feel some of seed still leaking out and she wondered if she should take a shower anyway.

She decided to have a glass of wine instead. Halfway through it, she heard Dave's key in the lock and she braced herself. He came in and saw her sitting there and smiled.

"Hi."

"Hi," she said and decided in that second to go for it. She

put her glass down and smiled at him. "I just came from Carlos where he practically attacked me and now I'm all horny for you." She spread her legs. "My panties are a mess, but what I really need is another orgasm like the one you gave me yesterday."

Dave hesitated just for a minute. "Did you tell Carlos...?"

She shook her head. "No, I didn't. But when I told him about how hard I came with you, I think he kinda guessed."

He nodded and approached her. "I'm still feeling a little sensitive about it all, I guess."

"I understand. But, god, what you did to me yesterday! I'm still reeling from the power of it."

He got down on his knees in front of her. "Really? It was as good as it is with Carlos?"

"Better, I think, because I love you so much." She pulled up her skirt and showed him the soaked panties.

"Tell me what you guys did."

"I will, but you have to make sure we don't mess up the couch." She reached out and cupped the back of his head, pulling him down her crotch. He didn't resist at all. His mouth opened and he licked at her damp panties. She gave a small groan to encourage him.

"We need to get these off," he said and she lifted her hips in response.

"Don't get any on the couch," she repeated.

He pulled her panties down her legs and tossed them onto the coffee table. He quickly returned to her leaking pussy and fastened his mouth to it and began to lick.

"Oh, god, honey! That feels sooo good!"

He made love to that pussy, as if his tongue was his dick. He was past his distaste for Carlos's semen, it was as if the man's juices spurred him on. Barb stopped observing him and just started to enjoy herself. She felt another orgasm rise within her and it surprised her that her body could come again so soon after Carlos.

"Oh god, honey, oh my god," she moaned and grabbed her legs behind her knees and spread herself open for him. "Yes, yes, oh shit! I'm commmmmming!" She shook from the pleasure of it.

When she came back to her senses, she saw Dave stripping of his pants and plunging into her. She barely felt him, but she would never say so. Instead, she encouraged him by saying, "Oh, yes, fuck that sloppy pussy! Come in that messy pussy!"

Dave seemed to like it because his face contorted and he fucked her harder. She felt his hand drop down to help himself come and she kept up her verbal encouragement until he grunted and came in her.

She didn't know where it came from, but she said, "Quickly, now – clean up your mess before it gets all over the couch!" She was surprised to see him obey, licking up the seed he had just spilled until she was clean.

He pulled back and looked up at her, suddenly realizing what he had done. "Please don't tell Carlos," he said.

She nodded, thinking, *Too late!* "I won't," she lied. "This will be our little secret."

He got up and went into the kitchen. He returned with a beer and took a long swallow, no doubt to wash away the taste of Carlos in his mouth. Barb had a sudden vision of Dave on his knees, taking Carlos's big cock into his mouth, making him come. Her pussy throbbed. She closed her eyes and shook the image away.

"You okay?" He asked.

"Yes! It was great! Thank you so much!"

He shrugged. "I know it wasn't as good as with Carlos, but…"

"Oh no! It was wonderful! You know I always come when you … do that. It's just so damn sexy."

Dave seemed pleased with himself. "Yeah, it's nice. I mean, I like being able to do that. I just… I don't know why I did it, you know, after *him*."

Or maybe it's because you really like being a little cuckold, she thought.

He finished his beer. "You want anything?"

She almost said no and reconsidered. "Yes, I would love another glass of wine." She handed him her near-empty wineglass.

He nodded. "Coming up." He returned a minute later with her glass half full and handed it over.

"Thanks." She wondered if she could push him a little more. "Honey? When you made me come, I think my toes curled so much, I pulled something. Would you rub my feet please?"

"Sure," he said and dropped down to her feet. "Which one?"

"Start with the left one, but both could use a little rub."

Barb sat there, sipping her wine and marveled at her husband, rubbing her feet like she was a princess. Or a queen. For all his protests, he seemed to be willing to play the role of a cuckold. She would like to talk to Carlos about it, but she had promised not to share Dave's little secret. Still, Carlos had guessed it already, hadn't he? Maybe she could talk around it. Or maybe…

She smiled. It would be nice to bring it all out into the open.

"Honey?"

"Yes?"

"I'm thinking of having Carlos over Wednesday night. Would you like to watch?"

He looked up, one foot held between both his hands. "Well, sure!"

"Good. Would you call him for me? See if he's free?"

"You… you want *me* to call him?"

"Yes. Tell him I'm missing his big cock and I want you there to watch us. See if he can make it."

"Uh… Okay." His face twitched.

"What's wrong?"

"Nothing… It's just that… I mean, didn't you just see him today? Do you need him again so soon?"

"Of course, dear. I think I could see him every day! But I'll take tomorrow off, so I'll be ready for him."

"Okay." He continued to rub her feet.

"Don't forget, hmm?"

"I won't."

Chapter Twelve

The next day, as Dave was leaving for work, Barb stopped him. "Did you call Carlos?"

"Um, no, not yet. But I will. I'll call him from the office."

"See that you do. I don't want him making plans with his other floozies."

He nodded and headed out. His stomach churned even as his dick grew hard. What the hell was wrong with him? He couldn't explain why it turned him on so much to go down on Barb right after Carlos had come in her – or why he always came so hard when he fucked her. He could tell right away how stretched out she was and he always had to use his fingers to bring himself off. There was just something about fucking – or licking – that messy pussy that drove him wild. Maybe it all the porn he'd been watching was starting to get to him.

And now he had to call Carlos to ask him to come over to fuck his wife? He wasn't sure about that. It was so embarrassing! Why couldn't she do that herself? He knew the answer to that – she liked making him a cuckold. He had asked her to go easy, but it didn't seem she was listening.

At the same time, it made him feel like he was participating. Wasn't it better than being left out? She could always go down to Carlos's apartment and leave him home. It was nice to be included. He did enjoy watching them together.

He arrived at his university office twenty minutes later and found no students waiting for him. Good. He had Carlos's cell phone number and he wondered if now was a good time. Carlos was probably at work already, busy with whatever novice stockbrokers did. Now might be the best because he wouldn't have much time to talk.

He dialed the number. Carlos answered right away.

"Hello?"

"Uh, hi, Carlos. It's Dave."

"Oh, hi, Dave. What's up?" He sounded brusque. Good.

"Barb … and I were wondering if you were free tomorrow night? She'd like to see you."

"Again? That woman of yours is insatiable, huh?"

Dave felt the heat rise in his cheeks. "Yeah, I guess she is."

"Well, I suppose I could stop by. On one condition, though."

Huh, thought Dave. *Now he's making conditions?* "What?"

"You shave her for me. All nice and smooth. Tell her that's how I like it."

"You mean…?"

"That's right. Tell her you have to do it. I like the idea of you preparing her for me. And take a picture, so I know it wasn't her who did it."

"Uh… well… okay…" That familiar feeling rolled through his stomach, part anxiety and part excitement. "If you say so."

"Great. Hey, I gotta go. I'll see you guys at seven-thirty tomorrow." He hung up before Dave could say goodbye.

He put down the phone. Taking a deep breath, he felt like a great weight had been lifted off of him. At least that was done! He wondered if Barb would make him do that every time she wanted to see their neighbor. He couldn't explain the mixture of emotions that roiled through him. He had read about "cuckold angst" but had never experienced it because he didn't see himself as that kind of guy. Yet he *did* eat Barb out right after she had been with Carlos. What was up with that? God, that had been so sexy! It made him rock hard and he had to fuck her afterward. He wasn't sure he was ready to embrace that part of his fantasy. He would just have to figure out where to draw the line. He was still an accomplished man, not like those wimps online! So why did it make him so excited to watch one of those video clips that featured a cuckold man wearing a cage or sucking on a big black cock?

Dave had no answer to that.

* * *

Barb was in the kitchen, making dinner when Dave arrived home. "Hi, honey," she said, "how was work?"

"Fine." He grabbed a beer and sat at the table, watching her.

She turned and frowned. Something was up. "What? Did you call Carlos?"

"Yes. He said he'd come by ... on one condition."

Barb stopped stirring and turned fully around to face him. "Oh, really?"

"He said I have to shave you... you know, *down there*."

Her mouth came open. "Shave me?" She couldn't resist the shiver that rolled through her body. "Really?"

"I guess he likes it that way."

"I guess so. Well, I guess we'd better do it then, huh?"

"Don't you feel it's ... a bit much to ask? I mean... it's kind of a personal demand."

"I don't mind if you don't. I've thought about it before, but you never seemed to care. But if that's what he wants... I'm game."

He nodded and sipped his beer. "Did you guys talk about this before? Like when I wasn't around?"

She shook her head. "No, but then, we were kinda busy. I

did trim it a couple times."

Dave nodded. "I noticed. I wondered if that was for him."

"It was for both of you! I just felt it was getting out of hand." She shook her head. "So, how else was your day?"

He chuckled. "Fine. How was yours? Any new lovers?"

She frowned. "Don't get jealous on me now, mister! We've got a good thing going here!"

"Sorry, that just slipped out. I guess I'm still trying to figure out how I feel about everything."

It surprised her that she could suddenly be so forceful with her husband. Maybe it was because he had been acting so submissive lately. "Sorry. Didn't mean to snap at you. I'm not a slut and don't say shit like that again."

"Sorry," he said again. He finished his beer and put it in the recycling. "So… when do you wanna do this? Tonight? Tomorrow?"

"Oh, I think tonight. I don't want to have fresh razor burns tomorrow. That might not be good."

"I'll be careful."

"See that you are! I'm not sure I trust you down there with a sharp object!"

"I'll use plenty of shaving cream. You have some for women, right? I doubt you want me to use my Barbasol on you!"

She smiled. "Yes, I have some." Another shiver ran through her shoulders and her pussy felt suddenly hot. "Dinner's about ready – would you set the table?"

After dinner, they sat around in the living room, but she knew he was stalling. He seemed lost in thought.

"Why didn't he just ask you to do it? Or do it himself?" he finally said.

"I don't know. I guess he wanted you to participate.'"

"Yeah. But isn't it enough that he's fucking my wife with my permission?"

"Maybe it's his way of making sure you're fully behind

it."

"Well, sometimes I'm not sure I am."

"Oh come on, you really seemed to enjoy the other day! I sure did!"

He blushed and shook his head. "I don't know what got into me."

"Well, don't stop! That was the best sex I've had in years!"

"Really? Better than with Carlos?"

"That's different. I mean, it was the best sex you and I have had in years."

"Oh." He stood. "Well, I guess we'd better get started, huh?"

She followed him into the bathroom. They both looked around the tiny space and then glanced at each other. "This isn't gonna work," he said.

She laughed. "Not hardly. Unless we both get into the tub! Let's do it on the bed. You bring a warm wet washcloth, my shaving cream and razor ... oh! And a small bowl full of hot water for rinsing. I'll go get myself ready."

She hurried off before he could complain. Her pussy fairly purred at the thought he'd be shaving it for Carlos. He must like his women to be smooth. She wondered if his other women were all shaved. Probably so.

She stripped completely naked and bunched up the pillows so she could see the process. She lay down and waited for Dave to bring it the equipment. It took him two trips. When he crawled between her legs, washcloth in hand, she warned him: "Don't you dare nick me!"

He looked up. "I won't."

He laid the cloth over her and she felt the warmth spread. He rubbed it in, getting her pubic hair warm and wet, and spread the shaving cream around. He pushed her legs wide apart. He picked up the razor and grinned up at her. "Here goes nothing!"

"God, this terrifies me."

"Just relax." Dave bent down and she felt him start shaving at the edges.

He was being very careful, she noted. He continued, moving from one side to the other until her mound was half bare. He paused and looked up.

"There was one more request he made."

"Oh?"

Dave pulled his cell phone out of his pants. "He wants a picture."

"What?! No way!" She sat up.

"He said it was the only way he could be sure that I did it and not you."

That stopped her protests in her throat. "You mean, like he doesn't trust us?"

"I don't think it's that. I think he just wants to see the process or something. It's his way of getting me involved."

She nodded and sat back. "Okay, but we're gonna erase that the second he's done seeing it!"

"I agree." He picked up the razor and said. "Maybe you should shoot it while I work."

She sighed. "Jeez." She took the cell phone and aimed while Dave returned to his duty. She snapped a pic and looked at it. Good, she thought. He could've been shaving anyone. There was no way to tell whose pussy was down there.

"Let me see." She showed it to him and he grinned. "Okay!" He returned to his work.

He looked so cute there, shaving carefully, like some kind of demented barber. Within minutes, he had finished and rinsed off the razor for the final time and used the wet washcloth to clean her pussy. "Whatdya think?"

She stared at her nakedness. She couldn't remember the last time she had shaved – probably back when she was in college and all the other girls were doing it. She had kept it up for a year or so, but grew complacent and allowed it all to grow back. When she met Dave, he didn't care, so didn't bother with it again. Now it fairly gleamed in the light.

"No nicks?" she asked him.

"None. I was careful."

She nodded. "You did a good job."

He bent down and gave her clit a tentative lick. "I think we oughta take it out for a spin."

"No," she said at once, closing her legs. "Let's save it for tomorrow."

Dave looked disappointed but he didn't argue. He collected the equipment and returned it to the bathroom. When he came back, she could see the small bulge in his pants.

"That turned you on, didn't it?"

"How could it not? Shaving a woman's vagina is very sexy. Come on, let's fuck." He started to strip.

"No," she said again, stopping him in mid-strip. "But tomorrow, you can do whatever you want – after Carlos is done."

He bit his lip and finally nodded. "Okay."

* * *

Barb acutely felt her bare pussy all day Wednesday. The way it rubbed against her panties made her wet and horny from about nine a.m. on.

God, she thought, *I should've done this years ago!*

At the gallery, she flirted with the male customers and succeeded in getting a verbal commitment from one man to buy one painting her boss had been trying to unload for months. Gustav was very pleased with her. He was the typical gallery owner: mid-fifties, salon-styled hair graying at the temples, an impeccable dresser – and gay.

"How did you pull that off?" he asked her.

"Oh, I don't know," she told him. "I just guess the right guy came in."

"The guy" had been a nice-looking man in his late forties wearing a suit and tie – and a wedding ring. He introduced himself as Bob. Barb, spurred by her naked pussy underneath her skirt, flirted shamelessly with the man, acting as if she might fuck him right there in the gallery if he bought something. When he expressed interest in the painting, she made sure she stood close to him while she described it and the artist, telling him it would surely go up in value if he bought it today.

Bob had turned and put his hand on her hip, asking casually, "And what kind of incentive can you offer?" He made it sound like he was simply asking for a discount, but she knew what he really meant.

She acted coy. "What kind of incentive did you have in mind?"

"Your phone number?"

"But I'm a married woman!" she protested as if she was shocked, shocked by his forwardness.

"So am I," he told her. "That doesn't stop me."

She demurred but when it looked like he might walk, she capitulated. She gave him her cell phone number but warned, "I'm not sure that this will do you any good."

In the end, she gave Bob a ten-percent discount – Gustav had said he would've given twenty just to get it out of his shop – and he promised to call. She had no interest in him really – Carlos and Dave were all she could handle – but her bare pussy seemed to be calling the shots today.

Every time she sat at her desk, she pressed her thighs together and thought of Carlos and their upcoming tryst. She wondered what he might say when he sees she was shaved for him. By the time she got home, she was beside herself.

She poured a glass of wine and paced, waiting for the clock to go around and for Dave to come home. She was two glasses into a bottle by the time he arrived and he noticed right away.

"Do you think Carlos is going to want you all drunk?"

"No," she admitted. "Sorry. I just got tired of waiting, I

guess."

"Don't peak too soon." He took the bottle and put it back in the fridge. "Just calm down. What's gotten into you, anyway?"

"It's the shaving," she admitted. "It made me horny all day!"

"Ohh," he said, grinning. "Guess it had the desired effect then, huh?"

"God! I nearly fucked a client today!"

"Really? Tell me."

She described the scene at the gallery and Dave's eyebrows shot up. "You gave him your number? What are you gonna do when he calls?"

"I don't know. I just wanted to sell a painting!"

"You'd better think of something to let him down easy."

"Yeah."

"Unless, of course, he has a big dick," Dave added.

Barb's eyes went wide. "No! It's not like that! It was just my naked pussy talking! Besides, he was white, so…"

"So you think his dick will be small, like mine? Is that what you mean?"

"I didn't say that! I just meant, I doubt he's hung like Carlos, that's all."

"Some white guys have big dicks, you know."

"I know. But I've found that a big dick isn't everything."

"Oh, so maybe you'd let this Bob guy use his tongue on you?"

The idea sent a shiver down her spine. "No!" she lied. "I'm not so easily … I'm not easy like that!"

"I dunno. You fell pretty hard for Carlos."

"That was different. I don't have any room in my life for anyone else."

"He might not buy the painting after all. Maybe he'll cancel the sale if you don't put out."

"Come on! It wasn't like that! It was just some innocent

flirting."

"So you say. I'd like to see what happens when he calls." He had a sudden thought. "Maybe you should ask Carlos about it."

"What?"

"You know, ask him if you think you should fuck him."

"I'm sure he wouldn't want that! My god, I'm not that kind of girl!" So why did the idea make her so wet all of a sudden?

Carlos was due at seven-thirty. While Dave straightened up the apartment and changed the sheets on the bed, Barb took another shower and got ready. She was too nervous to eat and insisted Dave fix himself something. He looked at her and shook his head.

"Jeez, Barb, you're acting like a schoolgirl!"

"Sorry – I'm just nervous." *And horny*, she thought.

At seven-fifteen, her cell phone rang. It was an unknown number and she looked up to see Dave smirking at her. "See, I told ya."

She answered it. "Hello?"

"Hi, Barb! It's Bob. Did I catch you at a bad time?"

"Sorta. I'm having dinner with my husband," she lied.

"Oh! I'm sorry. I was wondering if we could get together tomorrow for lunch and talk about the, uh, painting and maybe other paintings you can recommend."

"Oh! Sure! I can do that!" They set up a place and time and she hung up.

"See," she told Dave. "He just wants to talk about art!"

Dave made a noise with his lips. "Sure he does. He wants to get into your pants, I can tell."

"How? You didn't hear what he said."

"I just know the type. He'll start out talking about art and soon steer the conversation to how sexy you are. You watch."

"Well, if he does that, I'll just leave!"

"What if he ties the sale to sleeping with him? What

then?"

"I'm not going to sleep with him! I just want to sell a painting!"

The doorbell rang, interrupting their conversation. Barb jerked her head at Dave, who rolled his eyes and went to answer it. Carlos came in and Barb felt that familiar shiver from her pussy up through her nipples and into her brain.

God, this man just has to show up and I'm so wet I can't stand it! Or maybe that's from all this talk about how desirable Bob thinks I am...

"Hi," she squeaked.

"Did you do what I asked?" he said without preamble.

She nodded. He smiled and stepped close. He looked over at Dave. "Did you do it or did she?"

"I did it," he said, squaring his shoulders. "You wanna see the pic?"

He nodded. Dave pulled out his cell phone and found the image and held it up for Carlos. He smiled.

"Good."

"Now erase it!" Barb said and she noted that he looked to Carlos for a nod before he did so. Another sign he was deferring to the alpha male in their new relationship.

Carlos reached under Barb's skirt and touched the front of her panties. They were already damp. He rubbed his fingertips over the smooth material, nodding to himself. "Oh, yes, I can tell. Very nice."

Barb didn't move, wanting him to do more of what he was doing. When he pulled away, she felt the loss and her knees grew weak. She needed another drink.

"Dave, would you be a dear and get me some wine? Carlos, would you like a drink?"

He nodded. "Bourbon. Or whiskey. Neat."

Dave cocked his head at Barb. "Haven't you had enough already?" He turned to Carlos, "She's had two glasses."

"Okay! Okay! Just a splash, then!"

Dave nodded and went into the kitchen.

"How does it feel?" he asked her when he was gone.

Another shiver went up her spine. "It... very sexy. It... rubs me ... I mean, my panties rub against me and it gives me naughty thoughts. I'm sure that will go away in a day or two, though."

"Probably. But it's better, isn't it?"

"Yes, I'd have to say it is. I don't know why I got out of the habit. I used to do it back in college and right afterward. I guess it got to be too much trouble."

Dave returned and they stepped apart and accepted their drinks. Her husband had poured himself a bourbon, with ice. They sat and sipped quietly for a bit. Both Dave and Barb seemed to be waiting for Carlos to speak.

Finally Dave spoke up. "Did you tell him about Bob?"

Barb's face blushed red. Carlos turned to her. "Bob?"

"It's just a man I almost sold a painting to today. He, uh, seemed interested in me."

"Maybe that's because you were flirting with him!" Dave put in.

"Is that true?" Carlos asked.

"It was, you know, the panties! I mean, being shaved and all. It made me feel sexy. So I flirted – just to sell the damn thing that Gustav had been wanting to get rid of. But he insisted on getting my phone number – Bob, not Gustav. So he called tonight and he wants to have lunch with me tomorrow. I don't really want to go, but I'm afraid he might cancel the sale if I don't."

Carlos nodded. "So you led him on a bit and now you're trying to let him down easy?"

"Yes! I'm not interested in him. He's too old, for one thing. He's at least forty!"

Carlos tipped his head. "He's white, right?"

Barb nodded.

"So let him lick that nice smooth pussy of yours."

"I couldn't do that!" But her pussy throbbed at the very thought.

"But no fucking! That's mine now."

"Hey," Dave put in.

Carlos turned to him. "That's right. The only dick in your wife's pussy from now on is mine. You can use your tongue all you want."

"That's not the deal!" Dave protested. "She's my wife!"

"I know she is. But if your dick gets in there and ruins it for me, she'll have to find another lover."

They both turned to stare at Barb, as if expecting her to decide. She didn't know what to think – it was all so sudden. "Uh… Carlos, I can't very well ask my husband not to… have sex with me anymore."

"He can have sex – just not with his dick," he said.

"I'm not sure I can stop him! I mean, I sleep with him! He could just sneak it in."

"If he does, I'll be gone. You decide."

Barb wasn't about to give up Carlos. At least, not yet. She bit her lip and glanced at Dave. "I'm sorry, honey…"

He spun around in anger. "This wasn't the deal! I agreed to this only because it made you happy, but I'm not going to give up my husbandly rights! This little experiment is over!"

Carlos waited and watched Barb. When she didn't speak, he shrugged. "Too bad." He put down his drink and headed for the door.

"Wait!" she cried. Her pussy had been looking forward to this all day long. The sexy feel in her panties, the flirting, the anticipation. Would it all just fall apart so quickly?

He paused and said, "Decide."

Suddenly, she knew what he was doing. He had said so earlier, when he told her she'd have to be more assertive with her husband. She felt a calmness come over her.

"Dave," she said, "it wasn't really working anyway. I'm all stretched out now. You had to use your fingers to make yourself come. And I always come much better when you use your tongue, especially after Carlos has had me. So let's not kid ourselves. It's better this way."

His face grew red. He looked from her to Carlos and back again. Before he could speak, Carlos said, "We'll let you watch much more often, if that helps."

It was a bone and Dave took it. "All right. But this isn't over!" He headed for the kitchen to pour himself another drink.

Carlos smiled and took Barb's hand. "Shall we?"

She nodded and allowed herself to be led to the bedroom. He pulled the covers down and remarked on the clean sheets.

"Dave did that," she told him.

He grinned. "Great." He began to undress her and the clothes slipped easily from her body. She trembled and felt torn between her need for this man and her love for her husband. Would she cheat and let Dave slip it in later or would she stand firm? How would Carlos know either way? Could she lie to him?

He eased her down onto the bed and she watched as he got undressed. At that moment, Dave came in and sat in the chair, drink in hand. Barb tried to ignore him. Carlos climbed on next to her and took her into his embrace, kissing her face and breasts and making her hot. His fingers ran over her smooth mound and he murmured his approval.

"It's much better this way, isn't it?"

"Yes," she whispered, feeling her pussy grow wet and slippery.

Carlos spent a long time on foreplay until Barb couldn't stand it anymore. Her pussy wanted to feel his cock inside, to see how it might be different now that she was closely shaved. She rolled onto her back, reached down and grabbed his meaty member and steered it toward the vee of her legs.

"You want it?" he teased.

"God, yes!"

"Remember our deal. This is the only cock you get from now on. If Dave or anyone else gets in there, there will be trouble."

She nodded and felt the tip spread her apart. She moaned. It felt bigger, if that was possible. Without her hair to separate them, she believed she could feel every vein, every bulge of his skin, as impossible as that was.

"Oh god," she whispered. "It's sooo good."

Carlos grinned over her. "Yeah, baby, it's good, all right. I love fucking you."

He pulled back and pressed it in again and it slid smoothly until it was nestled fully inside. His short, wiry pubic hair tickled her bare mound and it made the sensations more profound.

"Oh fuck, oh my god!"

He began to stroke, slowly at first, until he reached a steady pace. Barb's legs came apart and she grabbed the backs of her thighs and pulled them out of the way, allowing every millimeter of his cock to enter her. Everything else faded away – the room, her husband, even the bed. She was all pussy and Carlos's cock was all the mattered.

"Fuck! Fuck! Fuck me!" she cried and felt the first orgasm ripple through her. "Yes!" Her body shook and tears came to her eyes it was so good. Her orgasms had no end, they just kept coming, one after another. She had never had anyone make love to her like this before, it was as if she was fucking for the first time.

Carlos began to speed up and she knew he was close. When he stiffened and she felt his cock throb, she shrieked and hugged him tightly to her until the sensations slowly faded away.

"Oh my god," she said when at last he pulled out and flopped down next to her. "Oh my fucking god."

"Oh yeah, baby, that was great. It's so much better without any hair in the way, isn't it?"

"Yeah." Barb belatedly remembered her husband and opened her eyes to see him staring at her pussy. She looked down to see the smear of fluids there and knew what he was thinking. But he was too embarrassed to do anything about it with Carlos there. He just needed a little push, she thought.

She nudged Carlos. "Why don't you go get me a glass of water and give Dave and I a little alone time?"

He got it at once and smiled. "Sure, baby." He got up and padded naked out of the bedroom.

"Come on," she told Dave. "You know you want to."

He licked his lips and glanced toward the door. "But he'll be back…"

"So what? He already knows – and I didn't tell him. He just guessed. Besides, don't you want me now?"

"I do! But…" He bit his lip. "I want to fuck you too."

"Hush now. We'll talk about that later. For now, just give me another one of your wonderful orgasms."

He came forward until his face was just inches away from the mess. Again he glanced at the door and said, "What if he comes back?"

"I think we have a few minutes. He knows we want to be alone."

That was all the convincing it took. Dave bent down and began to lick her pussy. It sent shivers up her body and she moaned and spread her legs for him. Once he started, he seemed to ignore everything else. He knew his technique and applied himself. Barb encouraged him.

"Oh yes, baby, that feels sooo good! Right there, yes, baby!"

She glanced up to see Carlos standing in the doorway, waterglass in hand. She smiled and waved him closer. He came in and put the glass down on the bedside table. Dave noticed him and stopped and his face turned pink.

"Ohh, don't stop, baby – it feels so good!"

Carlos tipped his head and left the room. Dave returned

to his duties. He soon had her buzzing and she felt another orgasm rising within her. Her cries were genuine and it encouraged Dave to continue. He seemed to have pushed the thought of Carlos out of his mind. When she cried out and held his head close, Carlos returned. His cock was semi-hard again.

"Move over," he told Dave and the poor man fairly scuttled out of the way. He stayed on the bed and watched the big man slip himself inside his wife again and he couldn't help himself. As he watched, his hand stole down to his pants, unzipped his penis and began to rub. They didn't pay any attention to him so he kept stroking his small cock until he spasmed and squirted his seed all over his hand. Without taking his eyes off the scene before him, he licked the mess off his hand.

When Carlos finished fucking his wife again, he got up and got dressed, leaving her gasping, her legs apart. He asked Barb, "Where and when are you meeting this Bob guy?"

She looked startled. "Uh, Anderson's, at one. Why?"

"No reason. But you have my permission to let him give you oral sex – just no fucking!"

"I'm not that kind of girl!" she protested and both Carlos and Dave laughed at that. Carlos gave Dave a wink and left. Dave licked his lips and eyed the mess Carlos had left. She really didn't need another orgasm.

"Oh, go ahead," she said, sighing.

Chapter Thirteen

Barb was nervous. She wanted to let Bob down easy, but not blow the sale. He had yet to pick up and pay for the painting. He had just made a verbal commitment. Gustav was eager to have the damn thing out of the gallery.

"Do you know how long this thing has been taking up space? At least five months! I have Alexander Richardson's work coming in and we've got to move some of these things!"

Barb told him she was meeting with Bob for lunch to discuss the sale and he nearly grabbed her. "Really? Why there? Why not just come here and pick it up?"

"Uh... I think he's kinda interested in me. Don't look at me like that – I told him I was married!"

"Ohh, I get it. He's probably trying to stall the sale so he can get into your pants. Oh, don't get all flustered, I'm not asking you to do that! But maybe you could encourage him just enough to get the sale done, hmm?"

Barb remembered Carlos's words and felt that familiar thrum in her pussy. "Maybe you could lead him on yourself, hmm?"

Gustav stood up tall. "I might, if he swung that way – anything for a sale!"

Barb had to laugh. "Well, I'll ask him and let you know."

"Just close the deal!" He paused and looked pained. "If

you must, you can give him an extra five percent off."

That would only be fifteen percent. "I thought you were willing to take twenty percent off!"

"I am! But don't tell him that unless you have to. Just close the deal!"

"Okay, okay."

Shortly after one, she hurried down to Anderson's and told the maitre d' she was meeting a man. She looked around and spotted Bob in a booth and went to greet him, her stomach in knots.

"Hi," he said, standing up. "So glad you could come."

"Of course. But it would have been much easier to meet at the gallery, wouldn't it?"

"That's such a formal environment. I thought we could get to know each other better."

She eyed his ring. "But why? I mean, you're married too!"

He gave her a weak grin. "Yes, yes, I know. We're both married and all, but you know how it is. Sometimes you just need some variety. Don't you agree?"

It was hard for her to lie, but she managed. "I'm happy with my husband."

He tipped his head. "Really? That's not what Carlos said."

Barb's mouth dropped open and she felt her cheeks grow hot. "What?"

"Carlos. You know Carlos, right? He certainly knows you."

She looked around and spotted her lover at the bar. Carlos grinned and raised a glass. "Fuck," she whispered. "What did he tell you?"

"We didn't have long to talk. But he did say that you belonged to him. That you and your husband have some kind of arrangement. I can guess! But he said if I closed the sale, I could sample your pleasures ... with my tongue."

"He… he said that?" She squeaked. "How dare him!" She tried to sound indignant, but her pussy felt like it was on fire. She wasn't sure if she liked being offered up. On the other hand, it sure cut through the bullshit. She had expected to spend a good hour trying to convince Bob to buy the painting and deflect any passes he made at her.

"So… do we have a deal?"

"No! I mean, I don't know. Uhh, how would this work, exactly?"

"Carlos said I could get a hotel room down the street. Once I've paid for the painting, we go there and … you know."

She didn't like the idea of going to a hotel room with the guy. How could she stop him from fucking her? "I'm not sure… I have to think."

"Look, I know how this sounds and all. I'm sure you think I'm a creep. But I've been married for twenty years and I just want to have a little fun. Your boyfriend there said it's possible if I don't expect too much and I treat you like a lady."

"And… and you're okay with … what he said? No … sex?"

He nodded. "Well, I would prefer everything. I mean, it's a big purchase I'm making here. But Carlos was… um, persuasive."

"Just a minute," she said, standing. "I have to talk to him." She walked over to Carlos, who was grinning at her. "What the hell are you doing?"

"Just having some fun. I know what the guy wants and he woulda talked your arm off trying to get into your pants. This way, you can make the sale and all it'll cost you is a little tongue action."

"I'm not a …" she lowered her voice and looked around, "prostitute."

"I know. But that pussy is mine now, right? I'm just offering another white guy a chance to clean it up."

"You mean… you're not going to…"

"No, I doubt he'd go for that. But he can give you an orgasm. I think you'd give up that for a sale, right?"

"I …" She shook her head. "I'm shocked that you think I'd do something like that!" So why was her pussy throbbing?

"Oh, stop it. I know you all too well. You're a little slut when you let yourself go. I'm just helping out."

"Oh? Helping out? And what if he … attacks me and I can't stop him? He's bigger than I am."

"Oh, I'd go with you two to protect you. He's already agreed to that."

"He… he has?"

"Yeah. Maybe he'd like to see the two of us in action."

"God." She closed her eyes. She turned and looked back at Bob, who smiled at her and held up his hands. He tapped his watch as if to say, "Time's wasting."

Her pussy made the decision for her. She could feel the heat from it and knew she was on the edge of a new adventure. For some reason, it made her feel desirable and slutty and … submissive. Yes, that was it. She liked being submissive as long as Carlos was around to protect her.

"You have to be there to protect me. Promise?"

He nodded. "That was the deal."

"Okay. But first, the sale." She returned to Bob. "Okay, here's the deal. We go to the gallery and you buy the painting – make it official. Then you and I and Carlos go to a hotel. And you have to pay for the room. Deal?"

He nodded and stood up. "Great. Let's go."

He dropped a twenty on the table and they headed out. She glanced back to see Carlos trailing behind. At the gallery, Carlos stayed outside. Gustav was all smiles when he spotted the pair. Bob wasn't a pushover, however and got his twenty percent discount after much haggling. He had wanted more, but Barb just hung back and tsked and tapped her watch.

"Okay, okay. Twenty percent off," Bob capitulated and

Gustav looked relieved. They moved to the side and handled the paperwork and when Gustav had the man's credit card info entered, he beamed at Barb.

"Okay, it's all done!" He winked at her and she knew she'd be getting a nice commission from it.

Now she was going out to earn it.

"Uh, Gustav, I need some time off this afternoon."

He stared at her. "Uh… sure." He glanced from her to Bob and back again. He wasn't sure what was happening, but he didn't want to ruin it. "Take all the time you need."

"Great." She left with Bob's arm draped over her shoulders. She could feel Gustav's eyes boring a hole between her shoulder blades.

Outside, they picked up Carlos and walked down to the hotel. Bob paid for a room and they all went upstairs. It was a simple room with a bathroom, not a suite. Carlos took Bob to a corner and talked softly to him so Barb couldn't hear. Bob's head moved up and down. Carlos separated and said, "I'm going to give you guys some privacy. Bob knows the drill. If he gets frisky, just call out and I'll come in." He held up the room key.

Now that it was happening, Barb felt very nervous. "You're… you're leaving? But you promised!"

"I'll be right outside, listening. Unless Bob wants me here…"

"No, no! I'll be fine. Don't worry. I'll treat her like a lady."

"Good. If you have any trouble, just call me," he told her. He waved and left. The door clunked behind him.

"Now," Bob said as he approached her. "I gather this is your first time? I mean, after Carlos?"

"Uh huh."

"How did you guys meet anyway?"

"He's a neighbor."

"Oh, I see. Well, he's certainly a, um, a polite gentleman!

So I guess you're like me. You love your husband but you just wanted to … experiment, right?"

"Something like that, I guess." It wasn't like that at all, but she didn't want to explain herself. She felt protective of Dave and his secret. "I'm not really this kind of girl."

"But you wanted to sell that paining, didn't you?"

"Yeah."

"So you were willing to compromise your morals – since you had already compromised them with Carlos."

"Look, this is getting a little too personal. I'm uncomfortable talking about it. If you want to … do what we agreed on, okay. But let's not talk about it, okay?"

He nodded. "I'm sorry – I didn't mean to pry. I was just curious, you know." He approached her and said, "So, how do you want to proceed? Would you like me to take off your clothes or would you…?"

Barb wondered if she could get away with just removing her panties. "How about this?" she said and sat on the bed and pulled her panties down and off. She hiked up her skirt and lay back, showing her bare pussy to him, framed by her stockings.

"Ohhh, you shave! How nice! My wife would never do that."

She nodded, not willing to explain to him that, up until yesterday, neither did she.

"But that's not going to do it. I want you completely naked."

"Oh, I don't know."

"It's the least you can do since I can't… you know."

She frowned and looked at the door. "You'll keep your pants on?"

He nodded. "Yes."

"Okay." She quickly stripped, feeling like a whore, which, she supposed she was. She lay back and Bob climbed on the bed and began kissing her. This made Barb feel uncomfortable and she pushed him away.

"Not that," she said.

He nodded and moved down her body. She allowed him to kiss her nipples and it did stir her ardor. When at last he moved down to between her legs, she gave him one last caution. "Remember, just the tongue. Carlos is right outside."

He nodded. "I got it." He bent down and began to lick her. It felt naughty and very sexy. She soon forgot about the circumstances and began to enjoy it. The man's technique was quite different than her husband's, but still very good. She closed her eyes and allowed the tingling to rise up from her pussy into her nipples. She reached up and pinched one and gasped from the sensations.

Being so naughty magnified every feeling. She was a whore, offering herself up to a stranger for a few pieces of silver. No, she clarified, she was Carlos's whore – she was doing this at his behest. She couldn't help herself. It allowed her to give up her scolding conscience.

"Oh!" she cried as her orgasm stirred. "Oh my!"

She couldn't believe it. She was going to come! Her legs came apart and she reached down to pull Bob's head deeper into her crotch. "Yes," she said, "right there!" His tongue worked its magic on her and she felt her stomach and legs begin to twitch. She lost rational thought as orgasm rose. It was very freeing, being a slut.

"Oh, fuck! That's it, OH MY GOD!"

She crested into her climax and felt Bob pull away. She was lost in the haze when she heard his pants unzip and looked down to see he had pulled his cock out! "Hey!" she cried. "No! Stop!"

"Come on, let me have a little fun too!"

His cock was only a little bigger than her husband's and she didn't want anything to do with it. Still, he was all worked up, she thought. She debated calling out for Carlos and decided to handle it herself.

"You can come on me, that's all," she told him.

He grimaced and grabbed his cock and began to stroke himself, aiming it at her stomach. But he couldn't help himself and he pushed the tip down and tried to enter her. She covered her pussy with one hand and cried out, "Stop!"

He grunted an apology and kept rubbing. In seconds, he had come all over her hand. It reminded her of Dave and she almost asked him to clean her up. The moment passed and she was grateful to see him grab a couple of tissues from the nightstand and hand them over.

"That was ... nice," he said. "Too bad we couldn't..."

She nodded. Now that it was over, she felt suddenly dirty. "Carlos!" she called out.

Carlos came in.

"We're done."

Bob quickly pulled up his pants and scuttled out of the room, muttering, "See ya," to the big man as he went by. Carlos said nothing.

He came over and sat down on the edge of the bed. "How was it?"

"My god! He tried to... Well, just for a second! I mean..."

"No, I mean, how do you feel about ... all this?" He waved a hand at the motel room and her naked body.

Barb had to stop and think. Part of her hated herself. She had acted like a whore, a slut and a very bad wife. But another part of her... She looked up at Carlos. "It was terrifying and dirty ... and very, very exciting. I really came hard! I know that sounds bad. I consider myself to be a good woman, a good wife, but... part of me wanted to fuck him." She shivered.

"It satisfies that secret part of you that you've kept hidden all these years. That part that was pushed down when you got married to a safe guy like Dave."

She nodded. "Yeah, I guess."

"It's part of being submissive. You did this because I pushed you into it, but it didn't take much of a push."

"Apparently not." She paused. "But I don't want to do this again! I'm not fucking guys for commissions!"

"Sure," he said, not sounding convinced. "But you feel alive, don't you?"

She nodded. "Does that make me a whore?"

"I would say, 'whore-lite'." He grinned. "As long as you're protected, it can be fun to let go a little, once in a while."

She glanced over at the bedside clock. "Oh! I should get back."

He nodded. "Me too. But since you're already naked…" He unbuckled his pants.

Barb, in her fevered state, didn't object. She welcomed the big man into her arms and his cock into her well-lubricated pussy.

Chapter Fourteen

Dave arrived home just before six and Barb was waiting for him. She hadn't showered since Carlos had come in her during their hurried coupling and she wanted to share the moment with her husband.

She was sitting on the couch, her panties crusty with Carlos's seed. She crooked her finger at him. "Come here, hubby."

He got a strange look on his face and walked toward her, putting down his briefcase and loosening his tie. "What's up?"

She spread her legs. "Guess who I saw today?"

He nodded and stared at the gusset of her panties. "Did you make a mess?"

"Uh huh. I saved it for you."

He went to his knees and pushed her skirt out of the way. "You've been a very bad girl," he said, licking his lips. "Very bad."

"I know. And I'm tender too. He was rough on me today."

"I thought you guys both had to work."

"We did. We met for lunch." *And that's not all that happened*, she thought.

"Well, I guess I'd better fix you up, then." He kissed the front of her panties, inhaling the scent of Carlos on her. "My god, it's pretty strong."

"You want me to go shower?"

"No, that's all right." He tugged at the waistband of her

panties and she raised her hips to help him. He slipped them off and let them fall on the rug. He bent down and began to tongue her. She couldn't help but compare his technique to Bob's and found them to be similar, but different in small ways.

"Oh my," she said and wondered if she should tell him about her adventures. Would he be angry or excited? She pushed the thought out of her head for now and just lay back and enjoyed the ride. Her orgasm rose up and she felt her body begin to shake and knew it would be a good one. It would also be her third sexual encounter of the day – with three different men, a new record! Just thinking about what a slut she was made it sweeter, if that was possible.

"Oh!" Her body trembled and she allowed herself to be bad. She wanted to tell her husband what a slut he had married and decided he might stop what he was doing. Barb remained silent, enjoying the sensations. The orgasm rose and she threw her head back, welcoming it.

"Oh yes!" she cried, pulling his head tighter into her. "Oh god, yes!"

Dave pulled away, his face smeared, his glasses askew. He had a crazed look in his eyes. Without a word, he pushed her back onto the couch and unzipped his pants.

"Hey!" she said. "That's not the deal! You have to ask Carlos!"

"Fuck Carlos," he said. "You're my wife!" He fell on her and she could feel his erect penis slip into her. After Carlos, it was a disappointment. He rutted with her for a few minutes while she hung on to him, not making a sound. He reached down to help himself – in essence, he was masturbating himself into her.

At last he gasped and she felt his discharge and she barked, "Hurry! Don't let any get on the couch!"

She was pleased to see him bend down and lick up his own seed. She pushed him away. "I'm going to go take a shower."

She showered, thinking about what Carlos would say about it – if she told him. Of course, she'd have to. That was the deal. She couldn't explain why she felt the need to confess – it just was there. Would he really leave her? She couldn't imagine it.

She dried off and got dressed and headed out. Dave looked alarmed. "Where are you going?"

"Down to see Carlos. I have to tell him."

"What?! You don't owe him shit! I'm your husband! I can make love to you anytime I want!"

"No, you can't," she said and left. She hurried downstairs before Dave could come out and try to stop her.

Carlos answered the door at once and cocked his head at her. He was dressed casually in sweat pants and a Giants top with the number 82 on it. "What? You didn't have enough?" He grinned.

"I felt obligated to tell you that Dave just fucked me. I couldn't stop him."

He gave a slow nod. "Okay. Let's go." He stepped out and shut the door behind him.

She didn't know what that meant. "Are you going to leave me?"

He didn't respond.

"Or hurt him? I don't want him hurt. He was just … I mean, he cleaned me up and he got carried away."

They reached her apartment and she let him in. Dave was sitting in the living room and he jumped up when he saw them. "What the hell?"

Carlos came in and stood over him. "We have an arrangement. I expect you to honor it. If you had asked me, I might've said yes, but since you didn't…"

"She's my wife! I can make love to her any time I want! You can't dictate terms to me!"

He was all puffed up like a grouper, trying to make himself look tougher than he was. She knew it was all show. He was just exercising his masculinity. He looked small next to Carlos.

Carlos nodded. "I won't punish you. I know you can't help it. But I expect better from Barb."

Dave's mouth sagged open. "What?"

Carlos turned and brought a straight-backed chair from the small dining room over and placed it down in front of the couch. He grabbed Barb by the arm and said, "Strip!" His voice was so commanding, she found herself removing her clothes at once. Dave started to protest and Carlos barked, "Shut up." He stopped, wondering what the hell was going on. Carlos held out his hand. "Give me your belt."

"What? Hell no!" He was starting to understand now.

"Give me your belt or I'll be out of your wife's life forever."

Barb looked up, half naked. "Dave, please! Give it to him!"

He unbuckled it and handed it over, his hands shaking. When she was naked Carlos sat down and pulled her down over his knees. He folded the belt over and addressed Dave. "Since this is your first offence, I'll only give her ten swats. But if it happens again, it will be twenty."

"No!" Dave said, "You can't!" He stepped forward as if he might interfere.

"No!" Barb cried from her upside-down position. "Sit down!"

Dave sat. He watched, pale and embarrassed, as Carlos gave Barb's bare bottom ten swats with the belt. They were hard enough to turn her bottom bright pink and leave a few welts. Barb was stoic throughout, just grunting with each blow. Tears poured from her eyes. When he was done, he dropped the belt and dumped Barb onto the rug. He stood.

"I trust we won't have another incident like that?"

Dave stared. He looked from Barb to Carlos and slowly

shook his head. He seemed defeated.

Carlos turned to Barb. "Tell him what you did today."

Oh god, she thought. "Uh… I was … a whore."

"What?!"

"I let that man who bought the painting – Bob – use his tongue on me. And … and I came." She felt ashamed saying it out loud.

"His … tongue? Did he fuck you too?"

She shook her head. "No! I wouldn't let him!" In her mind, she realized: *I wanted to.*

"Why did you do that?"

"Uh…" She glanced up at Carlos. The big man nodded. "Carlos wanted me to."

Dave's head whipped back and forth. "Carlos… What the hell are you doing? This has gone too far! I want this over with!"

"Sure," Carlos said. "All Barb has to do is say the word and I'm out of her life forever."

Dave nodded. "Barb?" He said, "it's time to stop all this."

She bit her lip. "I … can't."

"Why not?"

"I'm not sure I can explain it."

Carlos nodded. "I'll leave you two alone – I'm sure you two have some things to discuss." He left, closing the door gently behind him.

Barb got up and gingerly put her clothes back on. She felt ashamed and could barely face her husband. She went into the kitchen and poured herself a glass of wine. She brought Dave a shot of bourbon. He accepted the glass without a word, and said, "Well?"

She sat and described what had happened and how it had made her feel. "I don't expect you to understand, Dave. It was like an out-of-body experience. Like being allowed to be bad for the first time in my life. You know what I mean?"

"I'm not sure I do."

"I've always been the good girl, even back when I was a kid. My older sister was the rebel and I always wanted to be good to counter her somehow. I got good grades in school, I went to college while Beth ran off with that musician and broke my parents' hearts. After college, I looked around and found you, a very nice and respectable guy, and got married. My mom cried with joy! She loves you, you know."

"And what? You just married me because Beth was the wild one?"

"There's more to it than that, but yeah, I was being good. And I do love you. You're a very good man, but Carlos makes me feel alive in a way I can't fully explain. I wouldn't've done it if he hadn't been there to make me feel safe." She shook her head. "I don't expect you can understand. I'm sure this is just a phase I'm going through."

"I hope so! I mean, Carlos seems dangerous to you! What's next, whoring yourself out to his friends?"

She shivered and wasn't entirely appalled by the idea. She wasn't sure if she understood it herself. Carlos had said it – whore-lite. It was like, finally, at twenty-nine years of age, she was letting a little of Beth seep into her life. Her sister had turned out all right, too. She had married that musician and he had made a lot of money. Now she lived in Nashville with two kids and a dog in a big house. Her parents think maybe she wasn't so bad after all.

And the good girl is living a life that perhaps she didn't intend. It just sort of happened. Dave was safe and good and decent, but maybe a little bit boring. For the first time, Barb felt like she was living her life on her terms.

"If I want to have some adventures, you should let me." She took a sip of her wine and enjoyed the flavor. "I just want to be a little bit bad now and again. Carlos helps me and protects me. Besides, you seem to like it too."

He blushed and looked away. "Maybe I wanna be bad too, in a way. I mean, you say you've led the safe life, well, so have I. I never would've done ... all that stuff if it didn't excite me in a way. But I don't want it to take over my life! I have a reputation to uphold! I don't have tenure yet, so if it gets out that my wife is out ... doing things that the faculty doesn't approve of, it could reflect on me."

She nodded. "I understand. I don't want anyone to know about it, either. I have the feeling Carlos will grow tired of me and move on. Then we can go back to our regular lives."

"You mean our regular boring lives," he said.

She didn't say anything. He was right.

* * *

For nearly two weeks, Barb played it cool. She saw Carlos just twice – once at his place while Dave was at work and once at the apartment, with her husband present. Dave cleaned her up both times. He seemed to enjoy that part of it. He didn't try to fuck her – he had apparently learned his lesson. She did allow him to jerk off over her body and he cleaned that up too.

She wondered why Carlos hadn't been more demanding of her time and realized he was probably seeing his other women. She was still jealous. On Tuesday, she called him up as soon as she arrived home at four-thirty and asked if he was free. He was. She invited herself down. He agreed.

When he answered the door, he took her into his arms. She resisted and said, "We need to talk."

"Uh oh," he said, grinning. "You wanna call it off?"

"No!" she said at once. "I'm just trying to figure all this out, that's all."

"What's to figure out? You come down here when you want to get laid, that's all there is to it."

"I want to talk about ... what happened, you know. With Bob and all."

He nodded. "Okay. Talk." He waved her to a chair. She sat. He sat opposite her. "Would you like a drink? I bought wine."

She nodded gratefully and he poured her a glass of chardonnay. She took a good sip. "First, let's talk about your other women."

He sat back, surprise on his face. "Again? Why?"

"I don't know. Maybe I'm jealous. Maybe I'm just an insecure wife who wonders what her lover does when he's not fucking the shit out of her." She smiled.

"I told you – I only am seeing two other women. One married, one not."

"Tell me about the married one."

He nodded. "Let's call her Mary, although that's not her real name." He held up his hand. "And if she asked about you, I'd make up a name for you. I keep my secrets."

She smiled at that. "Okay."

"Anyway, she's thirty-five, has a kid. She only works part-time – mostly she's a stay-at-home mom. Her husband's kind of a work-a-holic who doesn't pay much attention to her, so she needed an outlet. I guess I'm it."

"How did you meet?"

"It was through my work, but I won't say more. It was about a year ago. I see her once every week or two, whenever she can fit me in around her schedule."

"Do you go there or does she come here?"

"Oh, I could never go there! Her neighbors would wonder about a big black guy coming up the stairs of her fancy apartment building! No, we meet at a motel near her home or rarely, if she can get away for a few hours, she'll come here."

"Do you do… anything unusual with her?" Unsaid was: *Like you do with me?*

He smiled. "No. Just straight sex. She's too uptight for anything like that. I'm sure she showers as soon as she gets home and never involves her husband. I'm just her sexual toy, I suppose."

"Do you wear a condom?"

He tipped his head. "Why? You worried?"

"No, I'm just curious."

"Yes, I do. She insists. She's not on the pill and she doesn't want to get pregnant with a black baby. That would kinda destroy her perfect life."

Barb nodded. It made her feel better to know that she was more involved with Carlos. "And the other one? Darlene?" She had wanted to add, "the floozy," but held off.

He nodded. "Yes. I told you about her."

"Tell me what you guys do together."

"You mean, do I spank her and whore her out?" He grinned. "No. She … likes certain things that I won't go into, but they're pretty harmless. She's just … very grateful, I guess. Now, out of the bedroom, we're not exactly compatible, but inside, we do just fine!" He grinned.

"What do you mean, you're not compatible?"

"It's just sex. We both know it and we're okay with it. Someday, she'll find another guy and get married and move on from me. Or maybe she'll get married and continue to see me. I don't know. I just know that when she comes over, we're gonna have a good time and that's it."

Barb nodded and took another sip of wine. "Does she make you wear condoms?"

He shook his head. "No. She's on the pill."

She felt a pang of jealousy, as irrational as it was. Or maybe it was caution. "Is she fucking other guys?"

"We don't really talk about it. I assume she might be, yeah."

"Doesn't it bother you? I mean, one of her other lovers might … have something."

"I haven't really thought about it. I suppose I should ask her."

"Yeah. I would like to know if you're … safe. I don't want to catch anything I can't get rid of!"

"Okay, so now you know. Satisfied?"

She nodded. "Okay. Now I want to talk about … what

happened, with Bob."

"I thought we covered that. You both liked it and were repelled by it and you kinda retreated back into your safe zone. I understood all that."

"Yeah, but now…" She shook her head. "I don't know."

"Ahh," he said knowingly. "You feeling 'safe' isn't where it's at."

"I don't know. I mean, it was dangerous. It was naughty. It was risky. But I felt really desirable, you know?"

"I find you desirable."

"Yes, and I love that! But there was something about it all that … attracted me. It was like a kid stealing a candy bar from a store or something. I've been the good girl and I got to be bad for just a moment and it was very exciting."

He nodded and stared at her.

"What?" She finally said.

"I want you to call Bob for me. Tell him that you really wanted to fuck him that day, but you were scared because he didn't have a condom. Tell him you'd like to see him again."

"No!"

"Yes," he said. "Be a bad girl again. But this time, tell him it'll cost him two hundred dollars to fuck you."

"My god!" Her pussy throbbed at the thought. "I can't do that!"

"Of course you can. And Bob is safe – he's not going to tell anyone."

"What… what about you? Will you be there?"

"If it's during a lunch hour, yes. You'll have to be … efficient."

"Maybe," she said. "I'm just not sure if I can do it."

"Sure you can. You came down here so that I would give you a push, to allow you to be the bad girl you want to be. And it will be Bob, whom you know, and it will have to be over in an hour, which is good. And I'll be there to protect you. It's perfect."

"I don't know…" she said, but she knew that was the good girl talking.

Carlos stood. "Enough talk. Either call him tomorrow or don't bring it up again."

She stood. "Aren't you going to fuck me?"

"No. Not until you call Bob."

Barb was escorted to the door, feeling atingle with conflicting emotions. But her pussy was definitely interested. Her very bad pussy that had a mind of its own.

Chapter Fifteen

She was nervous dialing the phone. Gustav was out front, talking to a customer, so she had the office all to herself, but probably not for long. She had put it off most of the day and it was three o'clock already and she was running out of time. She remembered what Carlos had said:

Either call him tomorrow or don't bring it up again.

She had decided several times not to call. It would be far easier that way. But she knew she'd want to talk it over with Carlos again and he'd be cross with her. He had been right – she wanted to be pushed. Her fingers shook as she dialed the number she had found on the computer. Robert Henderson, from Manhattan. She pictured him with his perfect wife and two children and shivered, remembering how eager he had been to fuck her.

"Robert Henderson." His voice startled her. He sounded brusque and efficient. His office voice.

"Uh… Uh…" For a moment, she thought about hanging up. Then she blurted. "It's me. Uh, Barb."

His tone softened at once. "Oh, hi! Uh, nice to hear from you." She could hear the question in his voice: *Why are you calling me?*

"I'm sorry to bother you at work… Is this a bad time?"

"No, I have a few minutes. What's up?"

"It's about… the other day. I feel I owe you an apology." In her mind, she flashed back to the day she offered Carlos an apology and look what that had led to!

"Oh, you don't have to do that. I'm fine."

"No," she said, her heart pounding and her pussy growing damp, "I need to explain. I really wanted to … do it, you know. I was just scared. But you really … excited me."

"I did?" He seemed pleased. "Well, maybe we could meet again."

"Yes," she said at once. "But this time, there's no painting hanging in the balance."

"No, we could just meet for fun."

"No, that's not what I meant. I mean, I got really excited, you know, offering myself up in exchange for you buying the painting. It made me feel like a really bad girl." Her face was hot she wondered if Bob thought her deranged. "And I would've, uh, let you, if you had brought protection."

"Really? Well, how can we fix this?" He was hooked now.

"I want you to pay me. And bring a condom. You know, like I'm … a bad girl."

"Ohhh, I see. Uh, how much?"

"Two hundred. It's a real bargain, considering."

"You haven't done this with anyone else?"

"Just Carlos. Oh, and he'll be there, just to protect me." She had a flash of insight. "You'd have to pay him."

"I see – like he's your pimp."

"Yeah." She couldn't believe she was being such a slut. "But you don't have to do any of this if you don't want to … I just… I thought you should know that I was really excited, being with you. And I thought you left thinking it was your fault or something. I know I led you on."

"Yes, yes, you did."

"So… are you interested?"

There was a long pause and then he said, "My wife isn't

putting you up to this, is she? Like a sting or something?"

"No, I promise! I don't even know your wife."

"I suppose you'd say that either way, but I guess I'll take a chance. I would like to see you again. I've been thinking about you, these past couple of weeks."

"Good! Uh, it'll have to be during our lunch hours. And I have to coordinate it with Carlos. You understand."

"Yes, but..." He paused. "You plan to do this again? With others?"

"Oh, I don't think so," she said, not sure if it was true. "You were a special case."

She heard the smile in his voice. "That's nice. Okay, how about Friday? It's usually pretty slow around here. I can get away at one for a good hour or so. That work for you?"

"Yes, but let me check with Carlos and get back to you."

"Okay. If it's a go, we'll meet at the Regis Hotel at one."

"Okay. I'll let you know by tomorrow."

She hung up, her body vibrating. How could she have done that? She should call him right back and say she had been kidding, it wasn't going to happen. But she didn't. Instead, she called Carlos and asked him if Friday at one worked for him.

"Yes, that's a good day for me. But I only have an hour for lunch unless I'm with a client, so you'll have to be quick."

"Quick is good." She paused. "God, am I really going to do this?"

"Yes you are," he said. "And if you don't, I'll spank your bottom until you can't sit down."

Her entire body shook from the memory of her spanking and her pussy clenched so hard she thought she might climax, right there in the office. "Oh god," she whispered.

Carlos laughed and hung up.

Barb didn't know what to say to Dave when she went home that afternoon. "Oh, hi, honey, listen, I'm going to be fucking some guy on Friday, you okay with that?" Or maybe, "Carlos is going to whore me out on Friday, but it's okay because the guy I'm fucking is gonna wear a condom."

She decided this was a conversation that needed a couple of glasses of wine first. She was on her second glass when he arrived home. For a moment, she wondered if she should say anything at all. *He doesn't have to know everything I do*, she thought. Then she remembered Carlos and knew he'd tell him if she didn't.

He caught her deer-in-the-headlights look. "What? Did you see Carlos today?"

"No, but I talked to him on the phone."

"Oh. Are you going to see him later?"

"No, not until Friday."

"Oh. So… what's up? You look pensive."

"I made a date with Bob."

He reared back. "Bob? They guy with the painting?"

"Yeah?"

"What for?"

"I want him to fuck me."

Dave's mouth dropped open. "Hey, what's this all about?"

"I'm just experimenting. Bob is pretty safe. He's married and doesn't want trouble, so it should be fine."

"Fine?! Listen to yourself! You're talking about fucking around like some kind of whore! I mean, Carlos was one thing, I could understand, you know, the whole black cock thing, but some stranger? I mean, he's probably got a tiny cock!"

"No, he doesn't. I've seen it, remember? I'd say it's about average." She meant: Bigger than yours. She took another sip of wine. "I don't expect you to understand. I'm not sure I do myself. It's just something I need to do to get it out of my system."

"I thought Carlos was for that."

"Carlos opened my eyes. He made me realize I've been a good girl who occasionally wants to be bad. In a safe way, of course! I'm not going out walking the streets. I'm just ... being a little bit bad. Just to see what it's like. And Carlos will be there to protect me."

"He's your pimp, you mean! God!" He stopped suddenly and asked, "Hey, are you gonna charge this Bob guy or is this a freebie?"

"I'm charging him. That's part of this whole thing. I'm gonna be a whore, just for an hour."

"My god! What happened to the girl I married?"

"She's still here. I'm just playing a role, just once. I'm sure I'll be appalled afterward and want to come home to my loving husband."

"I'm not in favor of this! Carlos was one thing, but this..." He shook his head.

"Don't worry – he'll wear a condom. It won't be like with Carlos." Meaning: You won't have to clean up after him.

Dave made a face. "Big whoop. I don't like this, I don't like it at all!" He stormed into the kitchen and she could hear him pouring a drink.

When he returned, she asked, "Come on, doesn't the idea titillate you a little?"

"No!"

"But you kinda like it when I see Carlos."

"Carlos is different. He's black, for one thing and that's ... kinda of a turn-on, as you well know. But if you're going out to spread your legs for some ... businessman, well, I'm against it! My god, I can't believe we're even talking about this!"

"It's all set up. I can't very well cancel it."

"Oh, no, you always do just what you want. Well, don't expect me to be here when you get home."

That surprised her. "But... where would you go? Would you really divorce me over this?"

"I don't know – I have to think! But I'm against it. It's a terrible idea."

That wasn't the reaction she had expected. She thought he might find the idea exciting, like he did when Carlos came into their lives.

"I don't understand why you feel you have to do this!" he continued.

"To tell you the truth, I'm not sure why I felt the need to do it, either." She decided not to tell him it was Carlos who pushed her into it. Well, a nudge anyway.

"Then why do it?"

"Come on, haven't you wanted to do something crazy once in your life?"

"Well, yeah, but that meant getting drunk and throwing up in the bushes, not this!"

"I guess we have different ideas of crazy fun. Don't worry, I'll be your good little wife again soon."

"No," he said. He took a big gulp of bourbon. "I'm not going to stand for it." He finished his glass and put it down. He grabbed his coat and headed for the door.

"Wait! Where are you going?"

"Out to think. Maybe I'll get drunk and throw up in the bushes." He slammed the door behind him.

Barb called Carlos at once and got his voice mail. She left a brief message, letting him know that Dave was angry and asked him to call. She hung up and paced the small living room, wondering if she had made a terrible mistake. It wasn't too late to call it off. It *was* a crazy, stupid idea. What had she been thinking?

So much for trying to be the bad girl, she thought. She had resolved to call Bob and cancel their Friday "date" when Dave came in. He had been gone just an hour. Barb was startled. He didn't seem drunk.

"You okay?" she asked.

He nodded. He clearly had something on his mind but

seem reluctant to tell her.

"What? What is it? Are you still mad at me?"

He looked embarrassed for the first time. "Uh…"

"Damnit, tell me!"

"I want to watch!" he blurted out and Barb almost laughed at him.

"You… you want to watch? Me with Bob? Uh, why?"

"I'm not sure I can explain it. Maybe it's to protect you, maybe it's…" He trailed off.

"Because it turns you on to see your wife with other men," she finished and he tipped his head and made a face.

Barb tried to imagine how that would work and couldn't. "I'm not sure Bob would go for that. It might impede his performance."

"I could hide… in the closet or something."

So now she had a Peeping Tom husband? Somehow, it seemed to fit the man he was becoming – or she should say, the cuckold. Barb remembered the layout of the hotel rooms at the Regis. "The closet is in the hallway by the bathroom and faces a wall. There's no place to hide where you could watch without being seen."

He nodded and looked dejected.

"I guess we could always invite him over here," she suggested. "You could hide in our bedroom closet." It faced the bed.

It was a crazy idea, one she was sure Dave would reject. But his face lit up. "You think he'd go for that?"

"Well, it would save him a hundred and fifty bucks, so yeah, I'd say he would. I'm not sure about Carlos, though."

"What does he have to do with this?"

"He's my protector."

"Pimp, you mean. Hell, I could be your protector."

"I thought you'd be hiding in the closet."

"Oh." He hadn't thought it through.

"It depends on if Carlos can get back here in time. He has

to do this on his lunch hour, you know."

Dave nodded. "Have you talked to him?"

"Not yet. I think he's on another date or something."

Just then her phone rang and she hurried to answer it. Carlos said, "Hey, baby."

"Oh, hi! We were just talking about you! Uh, Dave wants me to change my plans."

"He's against it, right?"

"Not at all – he wants to watch."

"Not sure how that would work with Bob. I don't think he wants an audience."

"It would if we did it here. Dave could hide in our closet. It's big enough. And you could do your, uh, protection thing while sitting comfortably in the living room, sipping a bourbon."

"Huh. I can't drink during the day, management would notice. But the rest might work. Have you talked to Bob?"

"Not yet. I'll call him tomorrow. But I'm sure he'd go for it because it would save him the hotel fee."

"Yeah, I can see that. Well, it's okay with me if it's okay with you guys."

She hung up, suddenly not sure how she felt about it. She would have preferred the anonymity of a hotel room. Having Bob know where she lives could cause problems down the road. "Do you think it's a good idea, having him come here?"

Dave pursed his lips. "Do you think he'd be a stalker or something?"

"No, he's married and doesn't want to rock the boat, but still…"

"You know him better than I do." He paused. "Uh, you gonna make him wear a condom?"

"I said I would! I don't know anything about his sexual history. He says he's been loyal to his wife, but the way he talks about their marriage, he could've been sneaking around before and not tell me about it."

Dave nodded. Barb wondered why he would ask that and suddenly got it. "Ohhh, I understand. You want to ... clean up, right?"

He flushed red. "No, of course not." She knew he was lying.

"I'll leave it up to you," she said. "If you don't want him to wear a condom, you tell me before he gets here, okay?"

He shrugged and let it go.

Chapter Sixteen

Bob had been all for the change of plans. "Great! That'll save me some money!" She gave him their address and confirmed the time at one-fifteen Friday, to give Carlos a chance to show up before Bob. She was nervous as a cat all week, wondering many times why she was doing this. The "bad girl" in her seemed to have fled and she was being tormented by guilt.

She didn't cancel because she had both Carlos and Dave looking forward to it. It was too late to back out, she decided. In some way, it was better to just go along. She could claim it was out of her hands, that she was a victim of her own circumstance.

On Friday, she went to work, her body aflame with desire and fear. She wanted to cancel many times, but stopped herself from reaching for the phone. *I'm going to be a prostitute*, she told herself. *I'm going to fuck a man for money while my husband and pimp watch over me.*

Somehow, the thought calmed her. At least she'd be protected. At twelve-forty-five, she told Gustav she had a lunch set up with Bob, who may be interested in buying more paintings. It was a lie, but Gustav bought it and she was out the door and in a cab in five minutes. She arrived home at five to and straightened up the place. She had made Dave change the sheets that morning, something he seemed almost too eager to do.

Dave arrived a few minutes later, looking breathless. He saw her worried expression. "Don't worry, honey, if anything goes wrong, I'll be right there."

"So will Carlos," she said dryly.

He nodded and looked at his watch. "Well, I guess I'd better hide, huh?"

"Wait." He stopped and turned around. "Do you want Bob to wear a condom?"

He hesitated. "Do you think he's, um, clean?"

"He's been married to the same woman for twenty years. I'd say yes."

He chewed on his lower lip. "He doesn't have to if you don't want him to."

"No," she responded. "If it's up to me, he'll wear one. If you want to, uh, participate, you'll have to tell me he doesn't have to." She was pushing him to see just how far down the path toward the full cuckold lifestyle he was willing to go. It would be useful later.

He took a deep breath. "He doesn't have to."

She nodded and followed him into the bedroom.

Dave had carved out a spot for himself in the closet, right by the edge of the sliding door. He crept in and adjusted the door to be open just a crack, facing the bed.

"Don't cry out when you come all over yourself," she said and he opened the door and made a face at her before readjusting it.

She heard the doorbell and checked her watch. Ten after. She wondered if Bob was early. She had told him to be here at one-fifteen, not a minute earlier. She answered the door to see Carlos standing there.

"Great! You made it in time." She felt an immediate sense of relief to see the big man standing there. "Come in."

"Is Dave here?"

"Yeah, he's in the closet already." She gave her head a little shake, thinking about how weird that sounded.

Carlos chuckled. "He's becoming quite the cuckold, isn't he?"

"Yeah, despite all his talk." She was about to tell him about the condom situation when the intercom buzzed, cutting off further conversation. Barb gave a long look at Carlos, squared her shoulders and took a deep breath. She pressed the button and made sure it was Bob and buzzed him in. A few minutes later, she heard the knock on the door. She opened it to see Bob standing there, holding a bunch of flowers. He smiled at her and looked over her shoulder at Carlos. He nodded at the pimp. He thrust the flowers at Barb.

"For you."

"Oh, how sweet." She took them and carried them into the kitchen. "I'll let you boys talk for a minute." A euphemism for "paying the pimp."

She peeked out from the kitchen to see Carlos and Bob talking in low tones. Bob's hand went to his wallet and a couple of bills passed hands. A visceral feeling rippled through her: It was official – she was a whore. She should be ashamed of herself, but all she felt was exhilaration.

She came out and said, "Everything okay?"

Carlos nodded. "I'll be out here if you need me."

She nodded and said to Bob, "Well, we'd better get started, huh? We only have an hour." She held out her hand.

He took it and she led him into the bedroom. It was an out-of-body experience. She was about to fuck this near-stranger and why, exactly? She was no longer sure. Part of her wanted to be the bad girl, but another part of her knew it was because Carlos and Dave both wanted her to do it. Did she still want to? She wasn't sure. She had seen the money change hands, so it was a done deal. All she had to do was lie down and spread her legs. It satisfied the submissive part of her.

In the bedroom, Bob closed the door and Barb didn't object. She started to strip, feeling self-conscious knowing that her husband was watching. Bob came forward, "Here, let me help you."

Her clothes came off of her easily and she lay back on the bed and watched Bob remove his suit and tie. When he was naked, he climbed over her and began to kiss her. For a brief moment, she remembered their last encounter and that old whore's adage came to mind: "Never kiss a client." She decided this was different now. She kissed him back.

They caressed each other and Bob moved down to take a nipple into his mouth. She moaned and tried to ignore the thought of her husband, watching her be a prostitute. His presence had a negative effect on her ability to perform. That was something she hadn't anticipated. She wasn't very wet and it worried her. Would he notice and be offended?

Bob kissed his way down her stomach to her pussy and began to lick. "Oh!" His technique was good and she felt her body respond. "Oh yes, that's nice," she said and spread her legs wider apart.

His efforts caused an orgasm to stir within her and she wanted to let it flow, but Bob had other ideas. He stopped and bent down to his pants and fumbled for something. Barb remembered her husband's request and put a hand on his shoulder.

"You don't have any diseases, do you?"

"No," he said, stopping to look at her. "I've only been with my wife." He paused. "You mean…?"

"You don't have to if you don't want to."

He nodded and asked, "How about you?"

She felt a brief wave of indignation and realized how ridiculous she was being. She had been fucking Carlos all this time! "I'm clean," she told him and hoped it was true. She wasn't so sure about Darlene.

He nodded and moved over her. His cock was bigger than her husband's, but smaller than Carlos's. It would be a nice test, she decided. He pressed the tip in and she groaned, half-faking it. Isn't that what whores do?

He began to move his hips, pressing more of his cock into her. "Ohh, that feels nice," she said. "Your cock is a nice size."

"Am I bigger than your husband's?"

"Oh yes," she said, knowing how that would cause cuckold angst in Dave. "Much bigger."

Bob wisely didn't ask if he was as big as Carlos. One look at the big man would've told him all he needed to know.

"And your husband doesn't know about this?" he pressed.

"Oh no, he'd probably divorce me."

"But he's okay with Carlos?"

"Carlos is different. He has a big black cock." As if that explained everything. Bob didn't question further.

He was fully seated within her now and as he moved, Barb felt this sense of wickedness that was delicious. She was a bad girl! A really bad girl! Sure, fucking Carlos probably also qualified her, but that was different. Now she was fucking a man bareback for money. Officially, she was a disappointment to her parents and a very bad wife.

God, what a turn-on!

She was pleased to be able to feel Bob's cock and wished her husband's was just a little bit bigger. A couple of inches thicker made all the difference! He had his own technique, going slow, adjusting his cock to hit her in all the right places. He kissed her mouth and her cheeks and nibbled at her earlobes, which she found to be very exciting.

Barb could feel an orgasm stirring and it surprised her. Didn't whores just fake it? She pushed the thought aside and let the sensations rise within her.

"Yes," she whispered, "Oh, yes!" It spurred him on. He moved faster and thrust deeper and she felt her climax approach. "God, fuck me! Fuck me hard, Bob!"

He grimaced and pounded his cock into her. She raised

her legs up and apart, encouraging him.

"Come in my bare pussy!" she cried. "Oh god!" She hooked her heels around Bob's legs and drew him deeper into her. "Oh god! It's so good!"

And it was good. Better than sex with her husband. She was living out her evil fantasy.

"Oh, god! I'm gonna come!" She couldn't believe it. He was making her come just like Carlos could. "Oh fuck!"

Bob kept pumping, his face a rictus of concentration. "Fuck!" he cried. "I'm gonna come!" He thrust hard into her and she felt his cock throb and knew he was shooting his seed deep into her womb. It was so nasty she came again. She clutched at him and let the waves roll over her until she was spent. Bob let go and rolled over next to her.

"Wow. That was great!" he said. "You're a great fuck!"

"Thanks. Was it worth it?"

"Oh yeah!" He raised himself up on one elbow. "When can we do this again?"

That stopped her. For some reason, she imagined this would be a one-time thing. Something she needed to get out of her system. But now, lying there and enjoying her post-coital glow, she wondered, *Why not do it again?* Then she realized, it wasn't entirely her decision.

"Uh, I'll have to let you know."

"Oh." He seemed disappointed, which made her feel *very* desirable.

"I'll call you and let you know. But it was really good, so if it were all up to me, I'd say yes. But you know, I have to check with my... with Carlos and all."

"Oh, right – your pimp."

She smiled. "He *is* my pimp, isn't he?" *And I'm a very bad girl!*

Bob rose and dressed. He checked his watch before bending down to kiss her. "I gotta go. It was great! Thanks." He left with the jaunty air of a man who just got laid.

She lay there and listened to the murmur of voices between him and Carlos. Then the front door closed and Carlos walked in just as Dave emerged from the closet, looking flushed. He spotted Carlos and seemed embarrassed.

Carlos ignored him and addressed Barb, who was still naked on the bed. If he noticed the white seed leaking from her pussy, he didn't say anything. "I gotta get back to work," he said and peeled a hundred dollar bill from the two he had gotten from Bob. "Here's your cut."

"Half?" Dave blurted. "She only gets half?"

Carlos frowned. "It's really none of your business. This is between me and her." He tipped an imaginary hat to Barb and said, "Let me know if you want to do it again. I've got lots of stockbrokers who would love to have a nice fine piece of ass like yours."

He left without another glance at Dave.

When she heard the front door close, she turned to look at Dave. "Well? I told him not to wear a condom, just for you. So don't just stand there!" It was becoming easier for her to order Dave around. She wasn't surprised when he crawled up between her legs without a word of protest and began cleaning up Bob's mess.

"That's a good boy," she cooed. "You do such a good job for me."

She lay back and allowed the sensations to rise up and overwhelm her. If she was supposed to feel bad, it wasn't happening. She felt very much in control of her life. Barb gasped when the small orgasm rippled through her and pushed Dave's head away. "Enough."

He unbuckled his pants and she stopped him with a stiff arm. "What the hell do you think you are doing?"

"Uh, I want to fuck you. You're so sexy right now..."

"Do I look like I need your tiny dick bothering me? Did you call Carlos and ask him? No and no." She closed her legs. "Besides, didn't you come while you were hiding in the closet?"

He swallowed. "No."

"Too bad." She looked at the clock. "I gotta get back to work."

She jumped up to take a quick shower, leaving Dave sitting on the bed, looking forlorn.

"My god! It was… I'm not even sure I can describe it!" she sat across from Carlos in his apartment, at four-thirty that same day. Barb was abuzz with emotions and Carlos was the only person she could talk to about it. She had floated through work and easily deflected Gustav when he inquired about her lunch with Bob.

"Oh, he's not sure he can afford anything else right now," she told him, thinking, *But he could afford to pay me to fuck my brains out!*

"So you don't feel guilty? Or ashamed?" Carlos asked her.

"I know I should, but I don't."

"How did Dave take it?"

She made a face. "He's become such a little cuckold! He cleaned me up after and really seemed to enjoy it."

"Oh? You didn't make Bob wear a condom?"

"No. At Dave's request, I might add."

"Huh. He's really getting into all this."

"Damn straight! And he wanted to fuck me after! I told him to take a hike. I said he had to call you for permission first."

"And he won't get it. But maybe we can use that somehow."

"Like what?"

"Oh, like turn him into more of cuckold."

Barb nodded. "And he said he wasn't into all that!"

"It was just his ego talking. Deep down, he's becoming quite the little sissy boy."

Barb imagined Dave wearing women's panties and sucking Carlos's big cock. "Ohh, do you think we could? Or should?"

"I don't know about the 'should' part, but we easily could. But let's put that aside for the moment. The big question is: Do you want to do it again?"

"With Bob? Sure. I'm just not sure about anyone else."

"What about with another black man?"

That stopped her. She stared at Carlos, her tongue slipping out to wet her lips, her pussy growing hot and damp. "Uhhh…"

"With a nice big cock…"

"I shouldn't."

"And I've decided to raise your rate to three hundred…"

"You still get half?"

"Yes."

She thought about that. "I'm not sure. Maybe I'm over it now."

Carlos shrugged. "Up to you. But I think you like being the bad girl."

"I do, but… I don't want to get arrested or anything."

"You won't. As long as it's controlled."

"And what about Dave? Are we going to let him watch all the time?" A twitch of distaste crossed her face.

"No," he said. "We'll go to the hotel. Dave can hear about it later."

"He'll be mad."

"I don't think it will matter, now that you're starting to take the upper hand with him."

She nodded. "Yeah." She shook her head. "I have to think about it. I mean, with Bob, I felt safe and all, but just to go out there and…"

"You wouldn't. I'd still be your pimp. I'd find your clients – discreetly – and I'd be there to collect the money."

"Of which you get half," she repeated.

He nodded. "That's the price you pay."

Barb pursed her lips. "I'm gonna have to think about it."

"Suit yourself." He stood and took her by the arm. She felt that familiar feeling of submission and found it incongruous with her growing control over her husband.

"What if I'm not in the mood?" she asked him.

He grinned. "Tough." Her pussy grew wet immediately.

They went down the hall together.

Chapter Seventeen

Two weeks later, Barb was in the Regis Hotel, legs spread, while a heavy-set black man pounded her with his fat cock. She had made him wear a condom, but that was the only concession. He slapped her bottom and pinched her tits. It was a total ownership of her body and she could do nothing to stop him from taking his pleasure. She was his whore for the hour.

Carlos was right outside the door, listening for any distress. Barb felt like a rag doll on the man's cock, which was every bit as big as Carlos's. His hands were like talons on her hips, thrusting himself deep into her.

Despite the abuse, Barb was having orgasm after orgasm and would've let the man do just about anything he wanted to her. Right now, he was biting her neck and she didn't care. At last, he grunted and she felt his cock spasm inside her. He pulled out and she could see the tip of the condom was full of his seed.

"Damn, girl! That was great!" He gasped for air and peeled the condom off and tossed it in the nearby trash can. He struggled to his feet and began to dress. "Wanna do it again next week?"

"I don't know," she said, not sure if she wanted another experience like that. Her pussy liked it, but it was rough on the rest of her body. "I'll have to talk to Carlos."

"Sure. Sure. But it was worth every penny, so anytime, baby!"

She smiled and watched him leave. Carlos came in and sat on the bed. "Well?"

"He was rough! You shoulda charged him more." That just came out. She didn't say, "I never want to see that guy again!" She just wanted more money. Typical whore.

"We can, next time. I'm sure he'd pay four hundred. The guy makes millions."

"Really?" Carlos had told her that most of the men he would find for her would be stockbrokers or bankers. It was his world.

"Maybe even more."

"Wow."

With that, Carlos peeled off a hundred and a fifty and handed them over. "You earned it," he said.

She accepted the money and looked down at herself. Her body was bruised and reddened. "Fuck!" She got up and looked at herself in the mirror. "My god! He gave me a hickey too! What will Dave say?"

"Do you think it will matter?" He snapped his fingers. "I have an idea…"

She turned. "Yeah?"

"You used a condom, right? But Dave likes it when you don't, so…"

He grabbed her and threw her down on the bed, unzipping his pants as he did so. She squealed and tried to fight him but he was too strong. She went limp when she felt his hard cock spread her pussy lips apart and sagged back on the bed. "You bastard," she said, but she didn't mean it.

He fucked her hard, for once not caring about her pleasure, only his own. It was what she needed, to be treated like a whore. Still, she managed a nice orgasm when she felt him erupt inside her. She clung to him until he finished and pulled out.

He stood and zipped up. "There, now you can tell your husband you fucked a black man and he left a present for him."

She shivered. "God! He'll be beside himself!"

Carlos looked at his watch. "I gotta get back to work. You okay here by yourself?"

She nodded. He kissed her and left. She sat on the edge of the bed and marveled at what a slut she had become. She looked down at herself once more. Her guilt returned, full force.

"This can't go on. Not like this," she whispered.

She showered at the hotel, despite her desire to save something for her husband. She just felt too dirty after that man had fucked her so violently. She could barely remember his name. Oh, right – Thomas. An upstanding stockbroker. He had seemed so polite until the money had changed hands. Then he was all over her. She shivered.

She looked at herself in the bathroom mirror. "Okay, it's been fun, but…"

She got dressed and left the hotel.

"You fucked another guy?" Dave was aghast. Barb wasn't sure if it was because she didn't let him watch or because she told him she showered right afterward.

"Yes. But I think I'm done now. It was fun and all, being a whore, but I'm not sure I need to repeat it."

"Well, good! I can't imagine why you did that in the first place!"

She shrugged. "I'm not sure either. I guess I wanted to see what it was like, being bad."

"You could've been hurt! You could've caught something!"

"I made him wear a condom."

He oozed sarcasm. "Oh. Well, good. That makes it all right then." He paused and asked, "Um, what about Carlos?

Are you over him too?"

She thought about it for a moment. "No. Besides, you kinda like it that I see him, don't you?"

He looked away. "I wouldn't mind having you all to myself again."

"Really? I'm not sure you could handle me any more."

"Oh, I see – now that you've experienced a black cock, you can't go back, is that right?"

"Something like that." She felt the need to reassure him. "Look, Dave – I still love you. That hasn't changed. I just need more in the sex department. We can just go on like we've been, with Carlos, okay?"

He tipped his head and gave her a half-shrug, a lukewarm approval. Then he said, "Can I still fuck you whenever I want to?"

She thought about it. "Um, no. I still want you to call Carlos first."

"Shit."

"You can always clean me up, though – your tongue is sooo talented now!"

"Great."

"Maybe we should get you one of those cage thingies – I hear that really helps focus the mind."

"What? No!"

"Oh, come on – I'll bet if I bought one, you'd want to try it out."

"No! That's... that's too much. I don't see myself like that." His voice had an edge to it, like he wanted to be talked into it.

"But it's okay to see yourself cleaning me up after my lover comes in me? Or Bob?"

He changed the subject. "What about Bob? Are you still going to see him?"

"I dunno." Truth was, she hadn't thought about it. "Maybe just once in a while."

"Shit – you said you were done with whoring yourself out."

"I did – but that was with Carlos's friends. Or at least the first one he brought me. He was too rough. He kinda mauled me."

"Let me see."

She wasn't sure she wanted to show Dave her marks. Then again, he *was* her husband. She unbuttoned her blouse and showed him the hickey and the red marks above her bra.

"Jesus!"

"I know. It was … intense." She shivered, remembering how it made her feel, like a complete whore. That was the point, wasn't it?

Dave came forward and took her into his arms. It was the most tender he had been in months. She felt safe. They hugged for a long time before separating. "I'm glad you're back," he said.

"I'm not all the way back."

"I know. But it's better than it was."

Later, in bed, Dave tried to make love to her. He rubbed himself up against her and begged her not to tell Carlos, that it would be "our little secret."

Barb was adamant. "You know what will happen if you do it! I'll get whipped!" The thought gave her a naughty thrill and she hoped he'd force himself on her. She couldn't explain why having Carlos whip her excited her so much. She could feel her pussy start to drip.

"Don't tell him!"

"You know I have to." She changed tactics. "This is why you need a cage, Dave – you can't control yourself."

He went silent and he stopped rubbing. "God, now you've gotten me all horny!" She said and pushed his head down.

He resisted. "Is this all I'm good for now?"

"Pretty much. I can't feel your cock anyway. You know

that."

He sighed, but didn't object. Soon he was licking her, driving his tongue into her and she threw her head back on the pillow and welcomed the sensations.

"God, yes!" she cried and pulled his head in tighter as her orgasm rocked her. "Oh my, that was good, honey!"

He crawled up over her and she felt the shaft of his hard penis rub against her. "Hey!"

"I'm not doing it! I'm just rubbing here a little!"

She gave in and let him masturbate himself against her pubic bone. "This is why you need a cage," she whispered. It seemed to excite him because he came a moment later, covering her mound with his juices. "Now, clean me up," she demanded, pushing down on his shoulders.

He sighed, but did as she asked. She smiled, thinking about how far he had come. Was it so much further to ask him to put on one of those cute cages? Or was she just being bitchy?

It took Barb two days to fully recover from Thomas's assault. She told Carlos he had ruined it for her. They had just made love in her apartment and were lolling on the bed. Dave was due home at any minute and neither one was worried about it.

"I think it's all out of my system. I don't want to whore myself out any more."

"Too bad. I had another guy all lined up."

"Really?" She felt suddenly desirable.

"Yeah. He woulda paid three hundred too. Oh, and Thomas said he was sorry and next time, he'd pay you five hundred and go easier on you."

"Wow." She had decided to get out of the business, but this was a lot of money to pass up! She didn't make much money at the gallery and Dave just brought in enough to pay the bills. Having another source of income –

She caught herself. "No. I'm not going to risk it."

Carlos shrugged. "Too bad."

"But I've been thinking about Bob…"

He grinned. "That white boy? Aw, you have a soft spot for him?"

"Yeah, I guess. Or maybe I just feel sorry for him."

"I'm thinking you don't need me there from now on. He seems pretty safe."

"Yeah, I guess." She rather liked having Carlos there to collect the money. "Wait – does this mean you don't get your cut?"

"If I'm not there, no, I guess not."

"Huh."

She changed the subject. "Oh! I think I've almost gotten Dave to agree to one of those cages!"

"Really? Figures."

"You think I should just buy one and present it to him?"

"No. I think you should buy it and put it on him. Hell, I'll hold him down if you want. He wants to be forced, I think."

"I dunno. He might really object."

"He really objected to you fucking me. Then he objected to cleaning up after me. Now he's halfway to being a sissy cuckold boy. You gotta keep the pressure on or he'll want to reclaim his masculinity."

"Maybe you're right. He humped my leg last night. He really wanted to fuck me and I told him to ask you. So he went down on me instead and then masturbated himself on me. But he cleaned it all up, so I wasn't too mad."

"Still, he should've asked me."

"That's what I told him." She shivered, thinking what Carlos might do. Her bottom twitched.

They heard the door open and didn't move. Dave walked into the bedroom and stopped short. "Oh, sorry…" he said and started to back out.

"Wait up," Carlos said. "I hear you nearly fucked my

woman here."

"Uhhh." He stared at Barb as if to say, *Why did you tell him?* "No," he said. "I didn't! I just... uh... rubbed up against her, that's all!"

Carlos sat up. Dave's eyes went at once to his thick cock, even flaccid it was twice his size. He jerked his eyes away. "Tell you what, Dave. I'll give you a choice. You can suck my cock – or you can hand me your belt and watch your wife get twenty swats."

"I didn't do anything!" he protested.

"You came, didn't you? You came on her without permission."

Barb recognized that Carlos was toying with Dave but her husband was too scared to see it.

"I'm sorry! It won't happen again!"

"I'm waiting – what's your choice?"

He looked from Barb to Carlos and down to his cock, then back to Barb. He seemed to stand up taller. "Go ahead, whip her."

"Dave!" Barb said. "How could you?!"

"Hey, you told him!" Dave retorted. "It coulda been our secret!"

"Okay, that confirms it," Carlos told Barb. "Order the cage."

"Wait – what?" Dave asked.

"Roll over onto your stomach," Carlos told her and she obeyed at once. To Dave, he held out a hand and barked, "Belt!"

He handed it over quickly, his hands shaking. "Wait... Maybe..."

"Too late now." Carlos took the belt, folded it over and slapped Barb's ass. She squealed as if it really hurt, but it hadn't been too hard. She was putting on a show for her husband. He hit her again. She cried out.

He hit her a third time and Dave said, "Stop!" He

dropped to his knees and waited for Carlos to turn and face him. He leaned in to kiss the big man's cock. Carlos sat back and watched him as he nibbled around the edges.

"You call that a cock-sucking?"

"Sorry." He took the tip into his mouth and began to suck on it. Barb watched, her ass burning and her pussy aflame. She wanted Carlos to fuck her again so bad she could taste it.

"More," Carlos said and Dave took more of the man's cock into his mouth.

It was by far the most erotic thing Barb had ever seen. Her pussy fairly gushed as she watched her husband give her lover a blow-job. What was even more surprising, Carlos's cock was growing in size, recovering from his recent lovemaking.

"That's it – get me nice and hard so I can fuck your wife again," he said and Dave nodded and redoubled his efforts. To Barb, he said, "Order it express so it'll be here in a day or two. If you need help with him getting it on, call me."

She nodded. Tears came to Dave's eyes but he didn't stop trying to get more of Carlos's cock down his throat. Finally, Carlos pushed him away and said, "That's good enough." He pushed Barb over onto her back and climbed between her legs. He turned to Dave, "Now, help put it in."

Dave's mouth sagged open, but he reached out and grabbed Carlos's cock and helped steer it into his wife's wet pussy. Carlos thrust himself deep into her and she gasped. Dave watched, fascinated.

He fucked her hard, like a man possessed. She came almost at once, just from the visual stimulation. Her body was tired, but it responded to him. When he stiffened and pumped his remaining seed into her, she clutched at him and never wanted to let him go.

Dave was still staring when Carlos rolled off and jerked his head at the mess. "Clean her up, boy," he barked and Dave, who was normally shy about doing his duty in front of the man, dove in and began to lick Barb's juices.

She lay back and allowed him to work.

"Get one of those steel ones," Carlos told her. "I think those are best."

"If you say so," she told him, grinning.

Chapter Eighteen

The cock cage came two days later. She called Carlos at once as soon as she arrived home and found the package outside her door. He told her he'd be down at six to greet Dave. Together, they'd make sure he put it on.

"Do you think we're going too far?"

"Hell no! The boy just wants to be talked into it."

Dave arrived at ten till six and she said she had a surprise for him.

"Really? What?" He had either forgotten about the item or had pushed it out of his mind.

"In a bit," she told him.

Then he got it. "Oh, no – I'm not doing that! That's for… I don't know, but it's not me!"

He went to fix himself a drink and downed it at once. He poured another. He was sipping it when the knock came at the door. Dave froze. "Is that…?"

"Yes." She answered it and let the big man in. He was still dressed in his suit. Dave suddenly looked small and contrite.

"Look," he said. "I didn't mean it, the other day. I was just kidding around…"

"Where is it?" Carlos asked and Barb went to fetch the package. They made a show of unwrapping it while Dave paced the living room.

"I'm not… You can't…" he sputtered.

When they got the steel cage freed from the packaging, Carlos held it up. "You think it's small enough?" He laughed at his own joke. He turned to Dave. "C'mere, sissy boy!"

"No! You can't make me!"

He sounded like a school kid, talking to the playground bully.

Carlos sighed. "Okay, I guess it's the belt then." He slipped it from his pants. Now Barb understood why he hadn't changed.

"My … no! You can't!"

"Sure I can. Your wife is mine to fuck or whip or whore out. I thought you got that." He folded over the belt and said to Barb, "Strip!"

She did, but she took her time, watching her husband as her clothes fell away. She could see the doubts and fears on his face. When she was naked, she asked Carlos, "Where do you want me?"

"Over the end of the couch," he said.

She got into position, her bare bottom raised up. She loved his ownership of her. He gave her a hard slap with the belt.

"Ow!" she cried. She looked back to see a welt forming.

Carlos gave her another, and another. Dave was weakening.

"Stop!" he cried. "Why don't you hit me, huh? Why are you picking on my wife?"

"Because that's the best way to get you to behave. Now, if you'll excuse me…" He gave Barb another slap with the belt and she yelped.

"All right, all right!" Dave capitulated.

Carlos nodded at Barb. "If you would do the honors."

She got up gingerly and rubbed her sore bottom. She found the cage and approached her husband. "Undo your pants."

Dave did so, but only after a long hard look at Carlos. A final act of defiance. The big man ignored him. Barb took one look and turned to Carlos, "He's kinda hairy. I think he should shave first."

"Good idea. Dave, go shave – unless you want Barb to do it."

"No, no – I'll do it." He scuttled off, his pants around his thighs.

Carlos looked at Barb as if to say, *Told you so*. She nodded in response.

Dave was gone a good thirty minutes. Barb got dressed and she and Carlos had time for a leisurely drink before Carlos grew impatient.

"Come on, boy! Get out here!"

Dave came back. His pants were pulled up, but still unbuckled.

"Let's see," Barb said and he reluctantly showed off his shaving job. His cock, which was small to begin with, now looked like a pale white worm. Barb stifled a laugh. "Much better," she said.

Carlos nodded. Barb took the cage and fitted it into place. His small cock seemed to shrink even further. Carlos handed her the padlock and she clicked it home.

"There!" She said, standing up and turning to Carlos. "What do you think?"

"Looks good. Now we don't have to worry about your little cuckold trying to hump you in the night."

Dave seemed dejected. He stared down at himself and seemed ready to cry. He looked up. "How long…?"

"Hmm, I haven't decided that," Barb said. "I guess it depends on your behavior."

"My … behavior?"

"Yes. I expect lots of attention. I want foot-rubs and clean-ups and … anything else I can think of. If you do a good job, I'll let you out now and then for a wank."

"But... can't I ever make love to you again?"

This time she let the laugh slip out. "Oh no! I've got Carlos for that!" When his face fell, she came forward and put a hand on his shoulder. "But your tongue is great! I still love that."

"Come on," Carlos said to Barb. "All this talk is making me horny." To Dave he said, "You come too – you can prepare us."

Carlos led Barb into the bedroom, Dave trailing behind, still holding up his pants. Carlos began removing his clothes. He nodded at Barb and she began to strip as well. Dave just stared at them, one hand holding up his pants.

"Come on, you too," Carlos barked. "Strip!"

Dave did, slowly. He was clearly embarrassed. He hunched over, trying to hide his new toy.

"Start with me," Carlos said. His big cock hung limply.

Dave's mouth sagged open. "Please..." he began.

"Come on, sissy boy! Get to it!"

Dave went to his knees, averting his eyes from his wife. He took the tip into his mouth and began to lick it. Carlos gave him a slap across his head and said, "You can do better than that!"

He redoubled his efforts and soon had half of the man's cock in his mouth, licking on it for all he was worth.

"Better," Carlos said, grinning at Barb. She stared, not believing her eyes.

His cock swelled and Dave was having trouble fitting his mouth around it. "That's enough," Carlos barked. "Now go prepare your woman."

Dave seemed grateful to be released from this duty and climbed up on the bed and knelt between Barb's legs. He used his tongue gently at first, then more forcefully until his wife was writhing on the bed.

"Okay, okay – that's enough. Now, help me stick it in."

He climbed over Barb, his big cock jutting out. Dave grasped it and helped steer it into his wife's pussy. His mouth was slightly ajar and he licked his lips. Carlos took over and Dave stepped back and watched as the big man fucked his woman. He reached down and tugged at his cage, fear and angst showing on his face.

* * *

Dave stared as the black cock spread Barb apart and made her cry out and she cling to Carlos, her legs wide apart in a vee, her body shaking. His throat became dry and he swallowed hard and licked his lips. The froth around Carlos's cock dripped onto the bed and Dave moved closer, right to the edge of the bed. He knelt down to get a better look. Now that he couldn't touch his cock, visual, auditory and olfactory inputs became paramount. He took in the sight of the cock pumping deep into his wife, the sounds of her voice and the slurping noises the cock made as it drove into her. He could smell her arousal and Carlos's musky scent.

God, he wanted to come in the worst way!

Carlos sped up and Dave bent down to see his balls slapping against her and knew he was close. His mouth began to water. Carlos stiffened and bellowed and Dave could see the muscles around his balls spasming as he pumped his potent seed into her. Barb cried out one last time and clung to him. For a long minute, he watched as this fat cock shot rope after rope of semen into her, some of it squeezed out around the edges.

At last, Carlos pulled out and saw Dave there, his mouth half open. "Me first," he said and rolled over and watched as Dave moved in to take his slimy cock into his mouth. "Good boy," he said. After a few minutes, he pushed him away. Dave's attention had moved to his wife's messy pussy.

"Go for it," Carlos said.

Dave hesitated just for a second before climbing up over Barb and bending down to clean up the mess. He used the flat of his tongue to get most of it and narrowed it to tease her clit and the folds.

"Oh, yes," she said. "Oh my, honey, you do such a good job!"

He continued, trying to wrest one last orgasm out of her. She lay back, her legs spread apart, sweat on her stomach and breasts and let him have his way with her. In a way, he felt he was fucking her, his own penis useless now, using his tongue like a cock, thrusting and probing and flicking at her. He brought his fingers up and slid two of them inside her. They weren't enough and he added a third. That brought a response from his wife.

"Oh! Oh yes! Fuck!" She crested into one last orgasm. It seemed small compared to the ones she had with Carlos, but Dave didn't care. He had made his wife come! That was all that mattered.

"Good boy," he heard Carlos say again and he pulled back, his face covered with juices. He immediately felt embarrassed and wiped his mouth with the back of his hand. "You can do that anytime she wants. Okay?"

He nodded. This was to be sex for him from now on.

"Uh… When can I be unlocked?"

Carlos shrugged. "That's up to her." To Barb, he said, "You should hide that key. Or maybe you should let me hold it for you."

Barb pushed herself up and leaned against the pillows. "I think that would be best. If it was here, he'd probably go searching for it or begging me. This way, he knows he'll have to ask you."

"Shit," Dave muttered. "You can't expect me to wear this all the time! What about work?"

"Do you take your clothes off at work?" Carlos asked him.

"No, of course not, but I have to use the bathroom. And if I go past a metal detector, it might go off…"

"When you use the bathroom, sit down to pee," Barb put in. "And I would avoid metal detectors if I were you. Might be hard to explain."

Dave's face fell. "This isn't fair!"

"Let's just try it for a week, okay?" Barb said.

Dave immediately felt better. A week he could probably do. He nodded.

Barb got up and slipped on a robe while Carlos dressed. Dave quickly dressed as well. Barb led Carlos out to the living room and they made a show of going through the packaging to find the key. Dave hung back and watched. Barb handed the key to Carlos, who put it on his keychain. He held it up and smiled. He kissed Barb and left.

Barb turned to him. "Let me see it."

He pouted. "Why? You saw it already."

"I want to see it again." She put her hands on her hips. "Unless a week isn't long enough for you."

He quickly unbuckled his pants and held the sides open. "See."

"No, I want it on display. Go take off your clothes."

"What?!"

"You heard me!" Her voice was sharp. "You can wear an apron while you fix dinner."

"You... you want me to cook? I don't know how!"

"It's time you learned. You can read, can't you? Get out a recipe and follow it. Look in the fridge to see what we've got. But first, fix me a glass of wine."

He stared at her as if he didn't recognize her anymore. "Why are you being so mean?"

"I'm not mean – I'm just taking my power. Now go."

Dave returned to the bedroom, not sure what had happened to him. He stripped and returned to the living room. She smiled when she saw his cage. He hurried into the kitchen and put on an apron and poured Barb a glass of wine. Then he began to look for recipe books.

Epilogue

Five months later, Barb and Dave and Carlos were enjoying their new, two-bed, two-bath apartment in a nicer neighborhood about six blocks from their old apartment building. The super was attentive and the elevator always worked.

Ostensibly, Carlos had one bedroom and Dave and Barb the other, although most of the time, Barb slept with Carlos in his king-sized bed. Dave slept on the queen-sized bed in the other room.

It had taken Dave a few months to adjust, but having one's cock locked up helped focus his mind. His original one-week trial had been extended several times by Barb, who grew cross at his whining and pouting. He had even gone to Carlos to beg for relief. Once. For that, he had had another week added to his time.

Matters came to a head one hot day in August, when they were still living in the old place. Barb had had enough of his wheedling and picked up one of his belts and slapped his ass with it. He grew angry and took it from her and proceeded to whip her legs and bottom. She immediately went downstairs to get Carlos and Dave knew at once he had made a big mistake.

Carlos had made him strip and lie on the bed. Dave had been too afraid to argue. Barb had fastened his hands to the bedposts with a couple of his ties and Carlos sat on his legs and let Barb whip him twenty times with the belt. He had broken down crying somewhere in the teens and by the time she was done, he was contrite.

"Now, I know that hurt, but it was for your own good," she had told her sobbing husband.

"I just wanted some relief! I've been locked up for over a month!"

"And why is that?"

"Uh… Because I was … um, complaining about… you know."

"That's right. Once you stop fighting me, you will get the releases you need!"

"I'll… I'll try."

"Good boy."

After that day, he had redoubled his efforts to please her. He kept their place spotless and cooked most meals and gave her orgasms with his tongue whenever she wanted. She released him a week later and let him come on her bare leg, which she immediately made him clean up. He seemed very grateful.

During the day, he was a respected assistant professor, teaching classes and mentoring young men and women. He hardly thought about his cock being caged – it was just part of him now. When he went home, he was the maid, the cook and on permanent fluffing and clean-up duty for Carlos and Barb.

He no longer thought it strange or gay to suck Carlos's cock, most of the time to prepare him for Barb, but sometimes just because the big man liked to exert his power over Dave. More than once, he had gotten too excited and come in Dave's mouth. Dave never complained, he just swallowed and waited for instructions. Barb, however, objected, telling Carlos not to "waste" his seed on her husband.

Carlos no longer saw Darlene, but he'd still go out on occasion to meet "Mary," his married woman. Barb had little reason to be jealous. Despite her claim that she was through with "the life," as she had come to call it, the lure of the extra money proved to be too much to resist. It had started with Bob, who became a regular visitor. He soon learned about Dave's secret and found it weird to have the man watch, so he'd make him wait in the living room. But he did like to invite the husband in after he had ejaculated in Barb, make him strip and let him clean up his wife, his cage dangling. He marveled at the strange relationship they had. As long as he got to fuck Barb now and then, he was happy to be a part of it. Bob's wife had no clue.

She charged Bob two hundred and told him it was a real deal, because Carlos's clients paid her four. Of course, she only got to keep half, so it really was the same to her. Barb saw about one client a week, usually at the Regis Hotel. Her second tryst with Thomas had been a nerve-wracking experience, but the big man was contrite and their love-making was much more gentle. It was almost a disappointment to Barb, who had braced herself for a real battle. When he tried to pay her the five hundred they agreed on, she would only accept four.

"Listen, the next time… you can earn that extra hundred. Just don't leave too many marks."

His face had lit up and he eagerly agreed. Carlos thought she had lost her mind, but he let her have her way as long as he could be there to monitor the situation. The next time, Thomas discovered her secret fetish – she liked to be spanked with his belt. Carlos knew at once where that had come from. She loved it when Thomas spanked her and immediately fucked her from behind, his wiry pubic hair rubbing against her welts. He was the only man who was allowed to do those things. Except for Carlos, of course. He found the belt helped her learn submissiveness.

Once Thomas and Bob became regulars, it was easy for Barb to accept the occasional client that Carlos found for her when she was feeling particularly naughty. She made them all wear condoms except for Bob, who was a special case.

The extra money she brought in allowed them to find a better apartment and the idea that Carlos would move in with them came up one night in late September. Carlos and Barb were sitting on the couch, sipping their drinks, while Dave was in the kitchen, making dinner, dressed only in his apron, his cute ass on display. It was a look Barb had decided she liked and made him cook like that all the time. Barb was telling Carlos they had been wanting to get out of this crappy apartment building for months and now felt they could afford it.

"You're right. I've been thinking of moving too."

"But you just got here!"

"I know. This was a good deal when I moved in, but I just got a raise and now I look around and think I can do better."

She perked up. "Oh, really? Well, we should find another deal like we've got now! I would love to have you in my new building. It's so convenient." She winked at him.

He nodded. "Yeah, if we can find two apartments we like that are open at the same time. Might be hard."

They sipped their drinks and suddenly turned to each other. "Hey!" they both said and laughed. "We could get a two-bedroom!" Barb said and he nodded.

Then she frowned. "What about your floozies?"

He tipped his head. "Oh, I think Darlene and I have run our course, and I only fuck Mary now and then. I'm sure you wouldn't object if I still saw her, right?"

Barb, who by then was fucking three other guys besides Carlos, realized how irrational her jealousy seemed. "I guess not."

"Good. So let's start looking."

"Do you think we oughta check with Dave?"

They both burst out laughing.

Within a month, they had found a place and moved in by

November first. Dave didn't seem too happy about the prospect, but he said very little as he helped them move. Carlos's brother Santana showed up to help and Barb didn't feel at all nervous to have the big, bald-headed man around, especially now that she could see Carlos in him.

Carlos took her aside and said, "Uh, Santana is happy to help, but …"

"What? Don't tell me he wants sex in exchange?"

He nodded.

"Fuck!" she said. "Now I'm giving it away?"

"It's a fair trade."

She sighed. "Okay – but not until we're done."

"Of course!"

Santana brighten up considerably after that and eagerly toted the heaviest loads and sweated off the most weight of the four of them. When they were all moved in and set up, Carlos sent his brother into shower. No one had told Dave about the arrangement and Carlos decided to leave that up to Barb.

"Honey," she had said while he was sitting on the couch, trying to rest. "I made Santana a promise to thank him for all his work…"

Dave frowned. "I thought he was doing that for his brother."

"Well, yes, in part. But he moved our furniture too."

"So… wait – you're gonna fuck him too?"

"Yes. But I'll be quick."

"Will he wear…?"

"Yes, of course. I don't know him very well."

He nodded. What else could he do? She knew he liked being unlocked for his monthly releases and he wasn't about to jeopardize it. He sat on the couch with Carlos, sipping beers, while they listened to Barb and Santana going at it in the bedroom. From the sounds of it, they were having a good time. At last, silence descended and a few minutes later, Santana came out, looking pleased with himself.

"Fuck me, that's a hot woman you got there," he said to Dave. To his brother, he added, "I can see why you wanna move in with her! Fuck! What a hot piece of ass to have around!"

Dave's face went red but he didn't say anything.

"Well, I gotta go."

"Thanks for your help," Carlos said, rising up to see him out.

"Sure. If you need any more help and Barb is the reward, just call me!" He barked a laugh and left. Carlos closed the door behind him. He turned to face Dave.

"So… here we are, all living together."

"Yeah."

"I'm sure it will take some adjusting."

"Oh, I'm sure."

An awkward silence stretched out.

"Guess I'd better go check on Barb – make sure Santana didn't maul her or something," Carlos said and left Dave alone in their new living room. Dave sipped his drink. After a few minutes, the sounds of love-making began again.

He sat and tried not to listen. Finally, he couldn't stand it and got up and went down the hall to Carlos's bedroom. The door was wide open. Like they didn't even care. He stood there and watched them fuck. Barb was on the bottom on her stomach, her ass raised up on pillows, legs wide apart, while Carlos thrust into her from behind. Barb was babbling her pleasure.

Dave tugged at the front of his pants, feeling the cage there and wondering when he'll be freed to beat off again. It was strange, but being locked up satisfied him in some way. It changed his thinking from his cock to his actions toward his wife and Carlos. Not only his tongue became important, but also his attitude. He had realized over the months that he liked being the cuckold, despite his early claims to the contrary. Barb had yet to demand he wear panties, but if she did, he would be ready to obey, just to please her. Pleasing her and Carlos had become the focus of his life.

Carlos bellowed his release and pulled out. His white seed had been whipped into a foam that started to drip. Carlos turned and spotted the man and jerked his head.

"Come on, let's not stain my new sheets."

Dave nodded and climbed up on the bed and fastened his mouth over his wife's pussy, swallowing the thick discharge. He could hear his wife murmuring encouragements. When she was clean, he pulled back and saw Carlos's cock semi-hard. With one look from the big man, Dave bent down and took it into his mouth and began to clean his wife's juices from it.

"Ohh, that's good. I think this new arrangement is gonna work out just fine," Carlos told him.